"You Should Dress Up More Often," Sinclair Said Gruffly.

"I don't really get the chance." Annie glanced across the room, where she could see a partial reflection in the mirror on the large wardrobe. She looked imposing in the long dress, and the dramatic blue brought out red-gold highlights in her hair. Sinclair's tall form blocked one half of the view, his broad shoulders in a striped shirt concealing the cleavage he admired. From this angle they almost looked like a couple, the distance between them foreshortened as if they were pressed together.

Like that could ever happen.

She attempted another carefree laugh, and again it vanished in the air, which suddenly felt hot and oppressive. Sinclair's frown deepened, and she shivered under his fierce stare. Words failed her as their gaze locked for a second, two seconds, three....

Sinclair's lips met hers with sudden force as his arms gathered her close. She melted, her mouth welcoming his and kissing him back with six years of unspent passion.

I'm kissing Sinclair.

Dear Reader,

I recently spent two years living in England, surrounded by history. We lived in a medieval barn where you could look up at curved ceiling beams that had held the roof up for centuries. From the kitchen window I could see the site of Roman baths, and I found stone tool fragments and shards of pottery every time I did any gardening. Even the oak trees were hundreds of years old, and I could imagine Roundheads and Cavaliers challenging each other under their spreading branches. All this made me want to write a book where history reaches into the present. At the heart of my new series, The Drummond Vow, is a lost chalice, a family heirloom that—if found—could hold the power to shape the destiny of three men, and the women who love them. I hope you enjoy this first book in the series.

Jennifer Lewis

JENNIFER LEWIS

THE CINDERELLA ACT

HARLEQUIN®

entertain, enrich, inspire™

Recycling programs
for this product may
not exist in your area.

ISBN-13: 978-0-373-73183-1

THE CINDERELLA ACT

Copyright © 2012 by Jennifer Lewis

www.Harlequin.com

Printed in U.S.A.

JENNIFER LEWIS

has been dreaming up stories for as long as she can remember and is thrilled to be able to share them with readers. She has lived on both sides of the Atlantic and worked in media and the arts before she grew bold enough to put pen to paper. She would love to hear from readers at jen@jenlewis.com. Visit her website at www.jenlewis.com.

For Jordan

One

"Are you sure this is safe?"

Annie tried to keep her eyes off Sinclair Drummond's enticing backside as he climbed the rickety wooden stairs to the attic.

"No." He flashed her a grin that made her knees wobble. "Especially with the curse hanging over our heads."

"I guess I'll take my chances." As his employee, Annie Sullivan could hardly refuse. She stepped onto the first rung of the hand-hewn stairs that were barely more than a ladder. They led up into the ceiling of the old barn, which was attached to the house so Drummond ancestors didn't have to face bitter winds howling in from Long Island Sound while tending to their animals. Now all it contained was an impressive collection of spiderwebs and brittle horse tack. The steps creaked alarmingly. "Have you ever been up here?" She hadn't, which was strange in itself.

Sinclair reached the top and pushed open a trap door. "Sure. When I was a kid. I used to hide up here when my parents argued."

Annie frowned. She couldn't imagine his quiet, dignified mother raising her voice, but she'd never met his father. He'd died in some kind of accident years ago.

"I doubt anyone's been up here since." He disappeared into the dark hole, and she climbed the stairs behind him with a growing sense of anticipation. A light snapped on, filling the opening with bright light. "I'm glad that still works. I didn't fancy searching by candlelight." Rain drummed on the shake roof overhead. His voice sounded far away, and she hurried to catch up to him. Her head cleared the entrance and she saw a row of uncovered bulbs dangling from the center beam of the windowless attic. Boxes and crates were piled along the sides, among disused tables, chairs and other, less identifiable pieces of furniture. The far wall was almost hidden behind a stack of big leather trunks bearing steamer labels. Despite the size of the room, very little of the wood floor was visible.

"So this is what three hundred years' worth of pack rats leave behind them. Where do we start?" Her fingers tingled with anticipation at rifling through the Drummond family's possessions. Which was funny, since that's what she did every day in her job. Of course dusting and polishing silver wasn't nearly as exciting as opening an old steamer trunk filled with mothballs and mystery.

Sinclair lifted the lid of a chest, which appeared to be filled with folded quilts. "Hell if I know. I suppose we just start plowing through and hope for the best." He'd rolled up his sleeves, and she watched his muscular forearm reach boldly into the fabric. "The cup fragment is made of metal, apparently. Possibly silver, but more likely pewter. It doesn't have any inherent value."

His shirt strained against his strong back as he reached deeper. Annie's heart rate quickened. Why did her boss have to be so gorgeous? It wasn't fair. She'd worked for him for six years and he'd only grown more handsome with age. He was thirty-two and his thick, dark hair didn't bear a single strand of gray, despite his two expensive divorces.

"And it's supposed to be cursed?" Annie suppressed a shiver as she glanced around. Her Irish ancestors would be crossing themselves.

"It's the family that's cursed, not the cup." Sinclair lifted his head and shot her a disarming glance. "Three hundred years of misery, which can apparently be lifted if the three parts of this ancient cup are put back together." He snorted. "I think it's a load of rubbish, but my mom is really excited about it. She's sure it will change all our lives."

"I was glad to hear she's doing better. Did they ever find out what made her so sick?"

"A rare tropical disease, apparently, similar to cholera. She's lucky to be alive. She's still quite weak so I've told her she should come out here for some rest."

"Absolutely, I'd be happy to take care of her."

"I'm hoping she'll come nose around up here herself. Then you won't have to do all the work."

Annie's heart sank a little. So she couldn't look forward to a summer in the attic watching Sinclair's broad hands reaching into mysterious boxes. She'd worked here for six years, yet on some level they were almost strangers. She loved being alone with him when there were no guests to entertain and she got a glimpse of a more relaxed Sinclair. The search for the cup seemed like a great opportunity to get to know him better. Instead, she'd be up here sweating under the rafters by herself. Still, the history all around her was intriguing. She walked over to a tall woven basket and lifted the lid. Coiled rope filled the inside, and as she pulled at it, she could imagine the hands that wound this rope in an era before machines. Everything around them must tell a story. "Why does she think the family is cursed? You all seem very successful."

Her own family would probably kill for a fraction of the abundance the Drummonds enjoyed.

"The Drummonds have done all right for themselves over the years. An old family legend has my mom convinced, however, that we're all cursed, which is why she got so sick." He lifted out a pile of clothes and she blinked at the powerful muscles in his thighs, visible through his pressed khakis, as he leaned to touch the bottom of the trunk. She startled as he suddenly looked up. "And why none of us can stay married for long." His blue-gray eyes shone with a wry mix of humor and remorse. "She's on a quest to unearth the three pieces of the cup and put them back together. She's sure it will turn things around for the Drummonds." He shoved the clothes back in the trunk and slammed the lid. "Of course I don't believe in the curse but I'd do anything to help her recover, and this has her really excited so I promised to help."

"That's sweet of you."

"Not really." He shoved a hand through his hair as he surveyed the piles of debris left over from former lives. "If it keeps her occupied she won't start nagging me to marry again."

Annie had watched grimly as he'd courted and dated his calculating and phony second wife. She wasn't sure she could stand to go through that again. "I suppose she's desperate for grandchildren."

"Yes, though you have to wonder why. Is it really necessary to carry the curse through to another generation?" His crooked smile made her smile, too. Of course his mother wanted grandchildren to spoil and fuss over. Though she wasn't likely to ever get any, if Sinclair's taste in women was anything to go by. She'd never met his first wife, but Diana Lakeland wasn't the type to risk her figure on a pregnancy. She'd married Sinclair for the wealth and prestige that made him one of New York's most eligible bachelors, then grown tired of him when he didn't want to jet around the world attending parties every night.

If only he could see he was wasted on those spoiled princesses. She couldn't tell him that, though. It was part of her job to be friendly, even intimate. But she also had to know where to draw the line between professional and personal, and never cross it.

She moved away from the basket of rope—more than enough to hang yourself with—and lifted a small wooden box from a high shelf. She opened the lid and found a cache of what looked like hairpins. Expensive ones, carved from tortoiseshell and bone. She wondered what Drummond damsel had tucked them into her tresses. "This does feel like looking for a needle in a haystack. Though it's an interesting haystack. Who did the cup belong to?"

"The Drummonds come from the Scottish Highlands. Gaylord Drummond was a gambler and drinker, who lost the family estate in a wager in 1712. His three sons, left penniless and landless, set out for America to seek their fortune. The brothers went their separate ways after their ship docked, and apparently they split up a metal chalice of some sort, each of them taking a piece. They intended to reunite the cup once they'd all made their fortunes. One of them settled here on Long Island, and built a farm where we sit today."

"I suppose that explains why you have such a large piece of prime waterfront real estate." The original farmhouse had been expanded over the years into a magnificent shingle-style "cottage" with bold gables and wide verandas. The old potato fields had been transformed into pristine lawn and lush orchards of apple, pear and peach trees. Once a sleepy village, Dog Harbor was now surrounded by the suburban sprawl of New York City. One ancestor had sold a field to a post-war developer to build tract housing. Sinclair's father had bought it back at great expense—houses and all—and turned it back into an emerald sward of grass. The cool water of the Long Island Sound lapped against a neat pebble beach about three hundred feet from the house.

Sinclair laughed. "Yes. The old homestead has matured into an excellent investment."

"What I don't understand is…how do you break up a cup?" It seemed hard enough to find a whole cup in this mess, let alone a piece of one.

"My mother says it was specially constructed to be taken apart and then put back together. She suspects it's an old communion chalice that was constructed like that so it could be hidden, maybe from Viking invaders or Protestant reformers, depending on how old it really is.

The story of the cup has passed down from generation to generation, though no one knows what happened to the pieces. My mom says she's tracked down the descendants of the three brothers, and contacted each of them about her quest."

"I think it's exciting. And a nice opportunity to reunite the family."

Sinclair shrugged. "I've never heard much good about the other Drummonds. We're all surly sorts who keep to ourselves." He raised a dark brow.

"You're not surly." She immediately regretted her pointless comment. The last thing she needed was for him to know she was smitten with him. "Well, not all the time, anyway." Now she was blushing. She hurried to a darker corner of the attic and pulled at a drawer. "Where do the others live?"

"One brother became a privateer raiding the East Coast and the Caribbean."

"A pirate?"

Sinclair nodded. "So the legend goes. His ancestors are still down there—or one of them, anyway—living on an island off the Florida coast. Since Jack Drummond's a professional treasure hunter I hardly think he'll help us find the cup."

"He might be interested in the family angle."

"I doubt it. The third Drummond brother got rich up in Canada, then went back to Scotland and bought back the family estate. His descendant lives there now. My mother hasn't been able to even get James Drummond to reply to her emails. She's tireless, however, so I'm sure she'll get through to him eventually, once she has her strength back." He lifted a box down from the top of an old armoire. "There aren't a lot of Drummond descendants out there. They don't seem to have had many children and a lot have died young over the years. Makes you wonder if the curse is real."

Was Sinclair cursed? If anything, he seemed to live a charmed life, dividing his time between his Manhattan penthouse and his other fabulous houses. She saw him for only a few weekends of each year, and maybe a couple of weeks in the summer. Just enough time to gaze dreamily at him but not enough to know his secrets. Did he have secrets? Passions and longings?

She tried to shake the thought from her mind. His inner life was none of her business.

"Some of this stuff really shouldn't be moldering away up here." Annie lifted a porcelain serving platter from its perch underneath another coil of rope. "I bet you could take this on *Antiques Roadshow*."

Sinclair chuckled. "And have them tell you someone bought it at Woolworth's in the 1950s." He stood over a big wood trunk, larger and obviously older than the steamer trunks piled high in several places. The inside appeared to be filled with folded clothing.

"Wow, look at that lace." Annie moved beside him, trying to ignore his rich masculine scent. She reached into the trunk and fondled the snowy cotton. "It doesn't look like it's ever been worn." She lifted the garment, which unfolded in a single soft movement, revealing itself as a delicate nightgown or petticoat. "Who did this belong to?"

"I have no idea. I confess to only ever rifling through the boxes with firearms and other guy stuff in them." Again his mischievous grin made her heart quicken. "I never touched the girlie stuff."

"Would you look at that." Setting the petticoat aside,

she peered into the large wooden chest to examine a richly worked bodice of green satin with red-and-gold edging. The needlework was exquisite and the material shone as if it had been woven yesterday. "I've never seen anything like it."

Sinclair pulled the garment from the trunk and held it up. Low-cut at the neck and with a tiny waist, the dress was an extravagant ball gown.

"It's stunning. And that blue one underneath it looks spectacular." She reached in and fondled a striking peacock-blue silk garment with tiny pearl bead accents. "These should be in a museum." It seemed a crime to leave them unseen in the dusty attic even a minute longer. "Let's bring them down into the house and hang them properly."

"If you like." Sinclair looked skeptical. Of course he probably only cared about finding the cup. "Sure, let's do it."

Had her face betrayed her disappointment so readily? His sudden change of heart touched her. She smiled. "Great! I'll carry as many as I can."

Sinclair strode down the narrow, rickety stairs without a moment's hesitation, despite his arms being filled with clothes. Annie teetered behind him, the heavy garments weighing her down and making her worry about missing her footing. "We can put them in the big wardrobes in the yellow bedroom. They're empty since your mom gave away those old fur coats."

She followed Sinclair back into the house and they laid the garments on the wide double bed. "I can't believe how beautiful this gray silk dress is. How on earth did they weave the silver and blue into the fabric?"

"Probably took someone years. Things were done

differently back then. Each item was a handmade work of art."

"I suppose ordinary people never even touched anything like this." She fingered the delicate fabric with its intricate ribbon detailing. "Unless they were helping madam fasten her corset, of course." That's what she would have been doing back then. Hey, she was still more or less doing it now, in a time when most women her age sat in plastic cubicles talking on the phone all day. She let her fingers roam inside the deep pleats at the waist and sighed. "What a stunning dress. I've never seen anything like it."

"Why don't you try it on?" Sinclair's deep voice surprised her. She'd almost forgotten he was there.

"Me? I couldn't possibly. They're museum pieces, and my waist isn't nearly that small."

"I disagree. About your waist, that is." His eyes settled on her waistband for a moment, making her stomach clench. Had her boss ever glanced at her waist before? She didn't think so.

Her heart pounded with excitement at the prospect of trying a dress on. Of course she could always wait until she was all alone in the house. But then someone would notice it had been worn, and she'd look foolish. What if this was her only chance? "Well…" She plucked gently at the peacock-blue evening gown. "I still don't think they'll fit, but…"

"That settles it. I'll discreetly turn away until you need help with the fastenings." He strolled to a tall arched window on the far side of the room.

Annie's heart quickened. She had an odd sense that a line between them was about to be crossed. Sinclair wanted her to try on the dresses. What did that mean?

Nothing, silly. He thinks it would be fun for you and he's humoring you. Don't get carried away. Really. This was foolish. She'd end up ripping a seam. "I'm sure they're supposed to be worn with all sorts of elaborate corsetry and I don't think—"

"Do you want to go back up and hunt for the cup?" He lifted a dark brow.

She hesitated, her fingertips still pressed against the rich fabric. A tiny smile tugged at her lips. "Maybe just one dress."

Sinclair nodded, a smile in his eyes, and turned away.

How sweet of him to let her try on a family heirloom. But which one? Without hesitation, she chose the rich peacock-blue. She held it against herself for a moment—the length was about right—and though the waist was narrow, it wasn't quite as tiny as she'd first thought. Maybe it would fit, after all.

She resisted the urge to turn and check on Sinclair as she unbuttoned her Oxford shirt. She knew him too well to imagine even for a second that he'd be sneaking a peek. He had women falling all over him wherever he went, and barely seemed to notice them.

She lowered her khakis and stepped into the crisp blue fabric. It was creased from being folded and smelled slightly of camphor, but otherwise looked fresh as if it were sewn yesterday. The tiny pearl beads tickled her arms as she pushed them into the short, puffed sleeves. The low-cut neck revealed a broad expanse of her white Cross Your Heart bra, so she quickly undid the bra and slipped it off through a sleeve. She had done up nearly half the tiny, fabric-covered buttons by the time Sinclair asked if she needed help.

"Just a few hundred more buttons." She smiled, already feeling like a princess in the luxurious gown. It fell to the floor and gathered there slightly, suggesting she should wear heels.

"Wow." Sinclair had turned and stood, staring at her. "Annie, you look spectacular." His eyes widened slightly as he surveyed her, slowly, from head to toe. "Like a different person." He crossed the room and fastened the last few buttons. "As I suspected, it fits."

"Odd, isn't it?" She fought the urge to giggle like a little girl playing dress-up. It didn't help that Sinclair's fingers were so near her skin that she felt giddy. "But why would we think people had different bodies two hundred years ago? They weren't so different from us."

"No, they weren't." Sinclair's voice was lower than usual. Done with the buttons, he moved in front of her again. His gaze rose over her neck and cheek, and she self-consciously tucked away a loose curl that had escaped her bun.

He frowned slightly. "You look pretty with your hair up."

"I always wear my hair up." She reached self-consciously for her bun.

"Do you? I don't know why I didn't notice it before." His gaze heated her skin.

"It's the dress."

"Maybe it is. You hide under your clothes and conceal the fact that you have a beautiful figure."

Her breasts swelled inside the fitted bodice. The cut of the dress acted as a bra, lifting things front and center. "Funny, I'm not sure I've ever had cleavage before." She tried to laugh, to hide her shock at her own bold statement, but the sound withered under Sinclair's stern regard.

"It suits you," he said gruffly. "You should dress up more often."

"I don't really get the chance." She glanced across the room where she could see a partial reflection in the mirror on the large wardrobe. She looked imposing in the long dress, and the dramatic blue brought out red-gold highlights in her hair. Sinclair's tall form blocked one half of the view, his broad shoulders concealing the cleavage he admired. From this angle they almost looked like a couple, the distance between them fore-shortened as if they were pressed together.

Like that could ever happen.

She attempted another carefree laugh, and again it vanished in the air, which suddenly felt hot and oppressive. Sinclair's frown deepened, and she shivered under his fierce stare. Words failed her as their gazes locked for a second, two seconds, three…

Sinclair's lips met hers with sudden force as his arms gathered her close. She melted, her mouth welcoming his and kissing him back with six years of un-spent passion.

His kiss was intoxicating as strong liquor. Annie's legs wobbled and she clung to him as their tongues wound together. Her nipples thickened against the lux-urious silk.

His scent was subtle, masculine and inviting. She'd never been this close to him before. His skin looked smooth, but now she could feel the roughness of his cheek as he nuzzled her. His fingers wound into her hair, loosing her bun, and a rough groan escaped his mouth.

A coil of lust unwound inside her. His desire, his need, was palpable. She could sense it vibrating in his

thick muscles and heating his tanned skin. His breath
grew hot on her cheek, further stirring the passion un-
folding in her belly.

What are we doing?

The thought seemed very far away, as if someone
else was thinking it. Her fingers climbed into his thick,
dark hair. It was silky to the touch. She could feel his
hands sinking lower, to cup her buttocks, and she arched
against him as he squeezed her. His breath came hard
and heavy, giving their kisses an air of fevered desperation.

I'm kissing Sinclair. The thought flashed in her brain
like a power surge. But instead of setting off alarms of
warning, it sent ripples of excitement dancing to her
fingers and toes. How many nights had she lain awake
imagining this moment?

His kisses were rougher and harder than she'd imagined, fueled by desire more powerful than she'd dared to
dream of. His hands fisted into the delicate fabric of her
dress, feeling for her body beneath. He pulled her closer
and his thick erection jutted against her. She gasped at
the sensation, such a bold sign of his desire—for her.

His name fell from her lips in a rasped whisper. She
pulled his shirt loose from his pants and reached for
the warm skin of his back. His muscles, thick and rop-
ing, moved beneath her hands. She'd seen him without
a shirt more than once, but never imagined the feel of
all that strength under her fingers.

He plucked at the buttons along the back of her dress
that they'd only just fastened. Her skin tingled at the
prospect of being bared by his hands.

Are you really going to let him undress you? Her entire body answered, *yes.* Sinclair must have been hiding

feelings for her the same way she'd been hiding them for him. Which was odd. She'd had no idea.

She giggled as he slid a hand inside the back of her dress. She'd already removed her bra and his fingers felt risqué and sensual against the bare skin of her back. More so as he lowered the dress and bared her breasts to his appreciative gaze. A lock of dark hair hung uncharacteristically in his eyes as he carefully pushed the dress past her waist. It seemed a shame to take it off after only a few minutes, but apparently it had already worked some kind of magic.

She stepped from the dress while unbuttoning Sinclair's shirt. She parted it and sighed when she saw his chest. Taut muscle with a slender trail of dark hair disappearing below his belt buckle.

Her nipples had stiffened to tight peaks, which bumped against his chest as she fumbled with the belt. The leather was stiff and Sinclair distracted her by nibbling on her ear. She could feel his fingers dipping below the waistband of her panties—if only she'd worn more sensual ones! She blushed at the thought of him seeing her oh-so-practical cotton granny briefs.

But Sinclair didn't seem to notice. His breath came hot and hard against her neck, in between ravishing kisses that stole her breath. His erection interfered with her efforts to unfasten his pants. When she finally got the zipper down she could see him straining against his boxers.

Her own breathing was labored and unsteady. Heat licked at her insides and she longed to press her naked body against his. With effort, they both pushed his khakis down past his strong thighs and he stepped out of them. They stood facing each other, a few scant inches between them. His body was perfectly toned, his stomach flat and hard behind his fierce arousal.

Annie swallowed. Were they going to make love right now? All signs pointed in that direction. Sinclair's eyes were closed, and his hands roamed over her body. Her skin stirred and sizzled under his touch. She felt the curve of his strong cheekbones and kissed him gently on the lips. How could such an ordinary day take such a wonderful and extraordinary turn? Maybe it was something to do with the mysterious cup.

Or was it the curse?

A dark shard of doubt cooled her skin like a sudden draft from a window. This man was her boss. On the other hand, the train had left the station. They stood naked in the fourth guest bedroom, the crumpled remains of their clothes at their feet. It was already too late to turn back and pretend that nothing had happened.

And she wanted nothing more than to take this surprising intimacy even further. She wondered if she should tell him she was already protected by the IUD she wore to ease her painful periods? She didn't want to spoil the delicious moment, so instead she kissed him again on the mouth.

"Annie," he groaned. "Oh, Annie." She almost exploded at the sound of her name on his lips. He wanted her as much as she wanted him. Her body ached to mesh with his and soon they were on the bed, him entering her with exquisite tenderness, while feathering kisses over her lips and groaning with unconcealed pleasure.

Annie wasn't a virgin. She wasn't all that far from being one, but she had some idea what sex was all about. Still, she'd never experienced anything like the intense sensations that rocked her body. Sinclair's fingertips pressed into her flesh as his mouth claimed her, licking and biting her with abandon until she gasped and squealed with pleasure.

She'd never imagined Sinclair having such an uninhibited side. He always seemed so straitlaced and conservative.

Sinclair moved with deft prowess, skilled at taking her to new heights of pleasure, and keeping her there until she was ready to burst into flames, then shifting position for an entirely new approach to ultimate sexual bliss. To see—and feel—him breathless with excitement and driven by obvious hunger for her, almost drove her insane with pleasure.

"Oh, Annie." Again he murmured her name, licking her lips and burying himself so deep she thought they'd become one.

"Oh, Sin." She'd imagined calling him that, fantasized about it being her pet name for him like he was some duke from one of her favorite novels. To hear the affectionate abbreviation on her lips, for it to sound so natural in the air, almost made her laugh with pleasure.

Sin. Surely that's what this was. But it felt so good it couldn't be entirely wrong. Sinclair claimed her mouth with a powerful kiss and her body burst into a convulsion of pleasure that left her shivering and gripping him.

Goodness. She'd never experienced that before. It must be the famous orgasm magazines loved to rave about. Sinclair released a deep, shuddering groan and fell against her, gasping for breath. Then, without a pause, he rolled them both over until she was on top and held her there, his arms fast around her and his eyelids shut tight.

"Damn," he said at last. "Damn."

Two

Sinclair wrapped his arms tightly around his lovely companion. Her strawberry-blond hair fell across his face. Her pretty, pale blue eyes looked at him shyly behind long lashes. He kissed her mouth again, her lips so soft and wet.

The sense of relief was extraordinary. Apparently going through his second divorce could set a man way off balance. He couldn't even remember the last time he'd felt this relaxed and at peace. He leaned forward and nuzzled her soft skin, with its pretty freckles. "You're a miracle," he whispered in her ear. Her cheek plumped against his as her lips formed a smile. The blissful weight of her body on his pushed him against the soft mattress, trapping him in the aftermath of such sweet pleasure.

He let out a long, deep sigh. Sometimes life could be so complicated, and you just needed to get back to basics. He let his fingers play in the silky red-gold hair waving softly about her cheeks.

"That was unexpected." Her voice sounded like music.

"Yes." His brain was too fogged for conversation. "And wonderful."

"It was. Though I hope my pot roast is okay. I totally lost track of the time."

Pot roast? Sinclair managed to find his wrist somewhere underneath her soft back and pulled it reluctantly out. "It's nearly five."

Sinclair's muscles were tensing up all over. Five in the afternoon. Pot roast overcooking somewhere. Present-day reality crept, unwelcome, into his mind. This delicious sylph in his arms was not a pre-Raphaelite fantasy maiden come out of the mists to entertain him.

She was his longtime housekeeper, Annie Sullivan.

"What's the matter?" Her soft voice filled with concern.

His stomach tightened as he lifted his arms from her. Had he really kissed her on the lips and pulled her into bed with him? His mind swam. He must have been in a psychosis of lust. His friends had warned him that going without sex for too long could do crazy things to a man's brain.

And now he was naked, sweaty and breathless, weighed down by the unexpectedly curvaceous body of the woman who polished his silver.

His head crashed against the pillow. In a way this was very stereotypical. Just the kind of thing his unsavory ancestors probably did with their staff. Another damning proof that he was no better than all the lying, cheating, philandering Drummonds who came before him.

Annie had noticed his change of mood. She, too, had stiffened and now pulled away, moving off him and to the side, with the snowy matelassé coverlet wrapped around her. Sinclair tugged the sheet up over his exposed flesh.

It was his fault, of course. "I'm so sorry."

Annie's cheeks were stained with red. She tucked her tresses behind tiny pink ears. He burned with shame that he'd taken such a good woman to bed without, seemingly, a moment's hesitation.

"Honestly, I'm not sure what came over me." Still reeling, he sat up and held his head for a moment. Was he in the grip of madness? Perhaps the same tropical malady that kept his mother in a delirium for nearly a week?

Contraception. The grim thought stabbed at his already pounding brain. "I don't suppose you're…on the pill." The unromantic utterance hung in the air like a poisonous cloud.

"Not the pill, but something similar. I won't get pregnant." Her silvery voice had shriveled to a tinkle. She climbed from the bed, back to him, still holding the coverlet about her naked body.

And what a body. He had no idea Annie was hiding such lush and inviting curves below her staid Oxford shirts and loose khakis. Desire snuck through him again, hot and unwelcome, and he pulled the sheet higher over his chest.

Annie had already tugged her rumpled shirt and khakis back on, and buttoned them with urgent fingers. He averted his eyes, cursing the demon of lust that had led him so badly astray. He'd better start exercising more regularly, and taking cold showers, to make sure nothing like this happened again. It was bad enough to be unprofessional in his own house, but what next, would he sleep with his administrative assistant, or the office receptionist?

A hushed curse escaped his lips, and Annie flinched. He startled, now aware that he'd added insult to injury. "I was cursing myself. I don't know what came over me."

"Me, neither," she muttered, tucking her shirt in. She picked up the blue dress from the floor, avoiding his gaze. "I'll hang this in the closet." Her voice was flat, devoid of emotion. Her lush body once again hidden under her practical attire.

Sinclair drew in a slow breath. He had to get out of here and back to Manhattan—stat. Annie left the room and closed the door behind her. He climbed out of bed and pulled his clothes back on, still in a daze of confusion. As he reached for his shoes, he saw her ponytail holder where it lay on the floor. It must have fallen out of her hair, releasing her locks as they...

He shook his head. How could this happen? He prided himself on maintaining control in all aspects of his life. He glanced at the pile of dresses where they lay on a wooden armchair, the lush fabrics lifeless, so different from how that dress had looked draped over her sweet hourglass figure.

He hurled himself from the bed with another curse. Clearly he was in the grip of temporary insanity. He'd better bury himself in work and make sure neither his brain nor his body had time and energy enough for such foolishness.

He dragged his clothes on and exited the room. The hallway was silent, the wood floor shining in mid-morning sun. Annie had tactfully disappeared, something she had a proven talent for doing. He also knew she would conveniently reappear if you happened to need her. She had almost magical qualities as a house-keeper.

Now he wished to hell that he didn't know about all the other qualities she possessed. He'd much rather not have felt the velvet texture of her skin under his finger-tips. He'd rest a lot easier not knowing that her breath tasted like honeysuckle, or that her eyes turned that par-ticular shade of sea-foam blue when she was aroused.

Rarely did he pack anything when he came here for the weekend. He had a closet full of casual wear that he pulled from. All he needed was his wallet and keys, which he found in their usual place on his study desk. Pocketing them with relief he strode for the side door, where his car stood ready to drive him back—at high speed—to normalcy.

The screech of tires on gravel confirmed what Annie had hoped for and feared. Sinclair was gone. She leaned against her bedpost for a moment, letting the odd mix of emotions flow through her. Her body still hummed and throbbed with the sensations he'd unleashed only a few minutes earlier. She could still feel the urgent im-pression of his fingers on her skin as he drove her to unknown heights of pleasure.

She closed her eyes and squeezed them tight. Why? And why now? Everything had been going so smoothly. She'd set up a savings account and a budget and was socking money away at an impressive rate, with the goal of buying her own forever home. Her own mini-Drummond mansion, where she could build her own self-contained world. She'd even found a fun sideline making crocheted cuffs and scarves to sell on the internet, with a view to being fully self-employed one day. Maybe she'd even own her own shop. All of this was largely possible because she was alone here 95 percent of the time, while the illustrious Drummonds lit up Manhattan or visited their homes in warmer or more fashionable places. This job was a dream for someone who simply wanted peace and quiet in return for some dusting and polishing. The fact that it paid well and came with a full slate of benefits was almost ridiculous.

And now she'd ruined everything.

She peered out the window toward the driveway, to see if she'd imagined the car leaving. No, the expanse of gravel was gray and empty, the old oaks standing guard on either side. Sinclair had sped back to his other life, and no doubt to all the women who awaited him there.

Drawing a breath down into her lungs, Annie stepped out into the hallway. Her own bedroom was on the ground floor, near the kitchen, away from the family suites. The house was empty and quiet as usual, but somehow the peaceful atmosphere had been whipped into a frenzy of regret. She headed along the downstairs corridor, where everything looked oddly normal, to the fourth spare bedroom—the one they hardly ever used—where they'd...

She pushed on the door gingerly, afraid of what she might find behind the polished oak. Her heart sank at the sight of the rumpled bed, one pillow flung carelessly aside and the sheet pushed to the end of the mattress. Her eye was drawn to the stack of rich Victorian dresses piled on the stark wood chair. The closet stood open where she'd hung the dress he'd buttoned onto her, then peeled off her. It looked so innocent draped there over the hanger. She could hardly blame a dress for what she'd done.

Two decorative embroidered pillows, scattered in the heat of their passion, lay on the floor. Where had the passion come from? She'd harbored fantasies about Sinclair almost since she first met him. Who wouldn't? He was tall, dark, handsome and filthy rich, for a start, but he was also such a perfect gentleman, so quietly charming and old-fashioned. A chivalrous knight in twentieth-century garb. Always polite and thoughtful to her, as well as his wealthy guests. It was impossible not to dream about him.

She picked the pillows up and automatically plumped them, then put them on the dresser. She could hardly put them back on this chaotic bed. She'd have to strip the sheets and wash them. She couldn't resist sniffing the pillowcase before she removed it. Faint traces of Sinclair's warm, masculine scent still clung to the white cotton. Her eyes slid closed as she let herself drift back for a second to the blissful moments when he'd held her in his arms.

Idiot! He probably thought she was a "fast woman." Which, apparently, she was. They'd gone from playing dress-up to the bed in less than five minutes. It didn't get much faster than that.

She shook her head and yanked the pillow from its case. Would she ever be able to look him in the face again?

Annie was hugely relieved when Sinclair didn't arrive the next weekend. She followed his instructions and continued sorting through all the old stuff in the attic. After a couple of days she'd found so many intriguing items that she decided to start an inventory. There was no sign of the cup fragment yet, but she found all sorts of other things that would probably make jaws drop on *Antiques Roadshow,* and it would be a shame for them to rot away for another three hundred years because no one knew they were up there.

The inventory also kept track of how much stuff she'd looked at, when it seemed like she'd barely made a dent in the piles of belongings stacked against each wall. She didn't want Sinclair to think she was slacking off now that she'd slept with the boss.

The memories made her cringe. He hadn't called, but then why would he? He'd already apologized for what he no doubt regarded as a disgusting lapse of judgment. What more was there to say?

Her heart could think of more things, but she told it to keep quiet. Sinclair Drummond could never have real feelings for her. In addition to inheriting money and estates, he'd started his own hedge fund business and made millions, which she'd read about in *Fortune* and *Money* magazines. As many articles as she'd read, Annie still didn't even fully understand what a hedge fund was. Sinclair had a degree from Princeton University, and she had a high school equivalency diploma. He'd been married twice, and she hadn't even had a serious relationship. They had literally nothing in common, except that they both slept under the roof of this house—her far more often than him.

Another week went by with no sign of Sinclair. Then the weekend loomed again. Friday evenings always made her jumpy. That's when the weekend guests would show up. Usually there was warning, but not always. She kept the house in a state of gleaming readiness, basics in the fridge, fresh sheets on the beds and fresh beach towels at the ready, just in case.

In the past she'd waited anxiously near a window, hoping that Sinclair would show up, preferably without some gym-toned investment banker girlfriend in tow. Today she chewed a nail. What if he did turn up with a woman? Could she greet him with her usual smile and offer to take their bags, as if she hadn't felt his hot breath on her neck and his hands on her bare backside?

When a car pulled in, her blood pressure soared. She immediately recognized the sound of Sinclair's engine. Fighting an urge to go hide in the pantry, she hurried to the window. *Please let him not have a woman with him.* Spare her that at least, until she'd had more time to forget the feel of his lips against hers.

She cringed when an elegantly coiffed blonde alighted from the passenger seat. *Thanks, Sinclair.* Maybe he wanted to let her know, in no uncertain terms, that there was no possible future between them. Not that his hasty and apologetic departure two weeks ago had left any doubts on that score. Should she greet them at the door?

She wanted to run out the back door and head for the train.

You're a professional. You can do this. She patted her hair and straightened the front of her clean pink-and-white-striped Oxford shirt. If he could pretend nothing had happened, so could she. Sooner or later they'd talk about it, and maybe they'd laugh.

Or maybe they'd never mention it. It would just be one of those wild, crazy things that happened.

Except that they usually happened to people other than her.

She pulled open the front door. "Good evening." Bracing herself against the supercilious presence of his newest lady, she nodded and smiled.

"Hello, Annie." His rich voice stabbed her somewhere deep and painful. "You remember my mother, of course."

Annie's gaze snapped to the elegant blonde. "Mrs. Drummond, how lovely to see you!" Thin as a rail and tanned to a deep nut-brown at all times of year, Sinclair's mother gave the appearance of being much younger than her fifty-odd years. She spent most of her time traveling on exotic art tours, and Annie hadn't seen her for nearly eleven months. Now, in her neurotic state, she'd transformed her into an imaginary rival.

"Annie, darling, I do hope I won't be a burden." Her big, pale gray eyes looked slightly glassy, and her tan wasn't quite as oaken as usual. "But the doctor says I'm out of the jaws of death and ready for some sea air."

"Fantastic." She hurried around to the trunk where Sinclair was retrieving their weekend bags. Then the rear passenger door of the car opened. She almost jumped. A tall, slender woman with dark hair climbed out, mumbling into a cell phone.

Annie's heart sank. Just when she thought she'd dodged that bullet, here was the new girlfriend.

She reached for one of the expensive bags, but Sinclair muttered, "I've got them," took them both and strode for the door. She quietly closed the trunk, painfully aware of how he'd avoided meeting her eyes.

"Mrs. Drummond, why don't you come in and have a cup of tea. If you're allowed to drink tea, that is."

She glanced back at the willowy young woman attempting to close the car door while juggling three large bags and her cell phone. It was probably in her job description to seize her bags with a smile, but she didn't have it in her.

"Annie, dear, this is Vicki." Mrs. Drummond indicated the girl, who looked up from her phone call long enough for a crisp smile.

Great. Vicki looked like exactly the kind of girl Sinclair didn't need. Arrogant, cold and demanding. Shame, that seemed to be the kind of girl he liked.

Maybe he deserved them.

"Hello, Vicki. Let me take that." Apparently she did have it in her, she thought, as she reached for the big silver bag with the D&G logo. Vicki, engrossed in her call, handed it over without a glance. Her sister always told her that she shouldn't be waiting on these people hand and foot like an eighteenth-century parlor maid.

With a suppressed sigh, and of course, a polite smile, she led the way into the house, glad she'd kept it polished and ready as usual. Sinclair had disappeared, probably up to his room. With a heavy heart she climbed the stairs with Vicki's bag in her hand. Vicki followed, laughing gaily into her phone. A glance into Mrs. Drummond's usual suite confirmed that Sinclair had already dropped his mom's bag on the bed. His room was the next one over, and she hesitated for a moment, wondering if Vicki's bag was supposed to go in there, too.

"You don't think I'm going to sleep with Sin!" Vicki's voice pealed down the hallway.

Annie wheeled around. Vicki strolled along the hallway laughing. "God, no. I don't think I even slept with
him when we were teens, but it's so long ago I can't
remember."

"Vicki can go in the blue suite," said Mrs. Drummond.

"Perfect. Suits my mood." Vicki stopped and rested a
bag on her hip for a moment, giving Annie time to take
in her skinny gray parachute pants and skimpy white
tank top, with a strange silver symbol dangling from a
chain between her high breasts.

Annie blinked. "Of course." So Vicki wasn't Sinclair's new girlfriend. Apparently she was someone
from his past.

"Vicki's an old and dear friend of the family. I'm
surprised you haven't met her before, Annie."

"It's been a long time since I've had the pleasure
of a visit to the Drummond manse," said Vicki, hoist-
ing her snakeskin clutch higher under her arm. "Funny
how the years have slipped past. I'm thrilled to be here
with you all."

Annie caught what might have been the barest possible hint of sarcasm in her voice, and her back immediately stiffened. Was Vicki here to take advantage of
their hospitality, then make fun of them? She certainly
didn't look like Sinclair's usual friends, with their carefully coiffed blond hair and cashmere twinsets.

"And we're thrilled to have you here, darling." Mrs.
Drummond walked up to Vicki, placed a hand on either
side of her head, and gave her an effusive kiss on the
cheek. Vicki's eyes closed for a second, and her forehead wrinkled with a pained expression. Annie stood

staring. She'd never seen such a display of emotion from Mrs. Drummond. "It'll be like old times."

"God, I hope not." Vicki shook herself. "I do hate traveling backwards. But it is good to be among old friends." She looked ahead down the hall. "Which is the blue one? I'm dying for a shower."

Annie jolted from her semifrozen state. "Sorry, it's this way. I'll bring fresh towels. Do you need some shampoo and conditioner?"

"I've got everything I need except the running water." Vicki's gaze lingered on Annie a teeny bit longer than was conventional. Annie's stomach clenched. She got a very odd—and not good—feeling about Vicki. Who was she, and why was she here?

For dinner, Annie prepared one of Katherine Drummond's favorite meals, seared salmon with blackberry sauce, accompanied by tiny new potatoes and crisp green beans from the local farmers market.

"How lovely! Obviously Sinclair remembered to tell you we were coming. I'm never sure if he will." Katherine shot a doting glance at her son.

Annie smiled, and avoided looking at Sinclair as she served them. Experience had taught her to be prepared for almost anything. And she did get real satisfaction from doing her job well. The room glowed with fresh beeswax candles handmade by a local artisan, and the windows sparkled, letting in the warm apricot light from the evening sun. If anything about the house was the least bit unwelcoming or unpleasant, it wasn't from lack of effort on her part.

She leaned over Sinclair to top up his white wine. His dark hair touched his collar, in need of a haircut.

Her breath caught in her throat as she remembered its silky thickness under her fingers.

An odd sensation made her look up, and meet Vicki's curious violet gaze. She turned away quickly and topped off Katherine's glass, then Vicki's. Had Vicki noticed her looking at Sinclair?

"It doesn't seem entirely fair for Annie to be running around topping things off when she made this lovely meal." Vicki's silvery voice rang in the air. Annie winced.

"She's right, of course," chimed in Katherine. "Annie, dear. Do bring a plate and join us. We're just family tonight, after all." She reached across the table and took Vicki's hand.

Vicki's eyebrows lifted slightly, but she held Katherine's hand and smiled. "You're so sweet."

Annie hesitated, humiliation and mangled pride churning inside her. She'd been enjoying this meal as the server, but sitting down at the table with them opened all kinds of uncomfortable doors. How would she know when to get up and bring the next course? Should she join them for a glass of wine, or stick to water so as not to burn the chocolate soufflés? "I already ate, thank you." The lie burned her tongue.

"Do join us anyway, won't you?" Katherine indicated the empty chair next to Sinclair. "I'm dying to hear how your investigations in the attic are going."

Annie pulled out the chair, which scraped loudly on the floor, and eased herself into it, as far away from Sinclair as possible. He hadn't looked up from his salmon. Had he even glanced at her once all evening?

Better that he didn't. She couldn't bear the thought of him looking at her with disgust and disbelief at his lapse of judgment. "I've gone through quite a few of the old boxes and trunks. I've made an inventory. Shall I get it?" She itched to get up. At least her notes would give her something to do with her fingers.

"No need for that right now. I'm guessing you haven't found the cup piece yet."

Annie shook her head. "I'm looking at every item I pick up to see if it could possibly be part of a cup, but so far nothing even comes close. I don't suppose there's a description of it?"

Kathleen sipped her wine. "Only that it's silver. It isn't jewel-encrusted. In fact we suspect it's not silver at all but pewter or some base metal. Odd, really, that something so precious to them would be so valueless."

Vicki leaned back in her chair. "It demonstrates an awareness of human nature. If it had real value, someone might have melted it down or pried the gems off to make earrings. By making it valueless to anyone but the family, they ensured its survival. Was it contemporary to when the brothers sailed from Scotland?"

"We don't know." Katherine took a bite of her green beans. She ate very slowly and cautiously, as if she wasn't sure whether the food was poisonous or not. Probably an effect of her illness, but it didn't help Annie's already frayed nerves. "The cup could be much older than three hundred years if it was passed down through the Drummond family before they came to America. No one knows where the legend about it first came from. When I first married Steven, Sinclair's father..." she looked at Annie "...his mother was still alive and loved to tell stories of the family history. She often wondered aloud whether it was time for us to put some serious effort into finding the cup." She raised a brow.

"Her own marriage wasn't a happy one, and all of her sons—including my own husband—were rather wild."

She looked thoughtfully at Sinclair for a moment. He appeared to be engrossed in cutting a potato. "Since then I've often wondered if finding the cup would somehow shift the course of fate and make life easier for all members of the family." She leaned conspiratorially toward Vicki. "The legend says it will restore the fates and fortunes of the Drummond menfolk, and I think as women we all know that makes life easier for us, too."

Annie felt a nasty jolt of realization. Katherine Drummond had brought Vicki here in the hope that she really would become a member of the family—as Sinclair's next wife.

A cold stone settled in her empty stomach.

"There are all kinds of interesting things up in the attic," she said quickly, anxious to pull herself out of a self-involved funk. "So far I've found everything from an old hunting horn to a huge pearl brooch. That's what made me decide to make a list. It would be a shame for so many special things to stay buried."

"Sometimes keeping things buried keeps them safe," replied Katherine with a slightly raised brow. "Especially in the age of eBay. Though I imagine Vicki might disagree."

Vicki laughed. "I believe in matching objects with their ideal owner."

"Vicki's an antique dealer," explained Katherine.

"Though some people have other words for it." Vicki lifted a slim, dark brow. "After all, value is in the eye of the beholder."

"I thought that was beauty." Sinclair said what were

possibly his first words of the whole dinner. A hush fell over the table.

"Aren't they really the same thing?" Vicki picked up her wineglass and sipped, gaze fixed on Sinclair.

Annie swallowed. Vicki oozed confidence, both intellectual and sexual. Of course Sinclair would be interested in her. She, on the other hand... "Let me clear the dishes." She rose and removed two of the serving platters.

"Value and beauty often have no relationship at all." She heard Sinclair's voice behind her as she exited for the kitchen. "Some of my most profitable investments have been in things that no one wants to look at: uranium, bauxite, natural gas."

"So you most value things that are plain and dull." Annie cringed as if Vicki's comment was directed at his interest in her. Not that he had any obvious interest in her. As far as she could tell, he hadn't looked at her at all since their perfunctory greeting.

"I most value things that are useful."

"What are we going to do with this son of yours?"

Annie scooped leftover potatoes into a plastic container to save for her own dinner.

"Well, Lord knows I've tried to loosen him up over the years, to no avail." His mother's voice carried from the dining room. "I think this legendary cup may be our only chance." The women's laughter hurt her ears. She was so clearly not a part of this tight-knit group.

And she'd better go retrieve the rest of the plates. She entered the dining room quietly. Conversation had shifted to some upcoming party. For a split second she felt like Cinderella, destined to help everyone get ready for the ball, knowing she'd never get to go.

She picked up the untouched plate of bread rolls, and couldn't resist sneaking the briefest glance at Sinclair as she lifted it off the table. When she looked up, their eyes met.

His cool, dark gaze sent a chill through her, at war with the swift, hot wave of attraction. Then he looked away. "I'm going sailing tomorrow." He spoke in his mother's direction. "I'll be gone all day."

"All the more time for Vicki and myself to make ourselves at home in the attic."

Annie's hands trembled, clattering the two plates she carried. Was she being ousted from the task of looking for the cup? She realized with a pang of disappointment that she'd come to feel quite proprietary about the attic and its trove of discarded treasures.

Which was silly. None of them were hers and they never would be. That blue dress hung in the closet a few yards away from where she stood, in the spare bedroom. For a few brief moments it had felt like hers, like she was meant to wear it. In retrospect it had been wearing her, and had turned her—briefly—into another person. Maybe it was better that she stay away from all this odd old stuff with mysterious powers.

She carried the plates into the kitchen, scraped them and put them in the dishwasher. Her ears were pricked for the sound of Sinclair's voice, but all she heard was the chatter of the two women.

He doesn't care about you. It was a momentary lapse of judgment. An act of madness.

"Annie." His voice right behind her made her jump. She wheeled around and saw him standing, larger than life, in the kitchen. "We need to talk."

She gulped. "Yes."

"Tomorrow." His eyes narrowed. Stress had carved a line between his brows. "When we can be alone."

She nodded, heart pounding. Sinclair turned and strode from the room, his powerful shoulders hunched slightly inside his starched shirt.

He'd been so taciturn tonight, barely joining the conversation. Was he thinking about her? She rinsed the cutlery and put it into the dishwasher. For a while she thought he'd simply pretend nothing had happened. He made no contact with her after they'd made love and two weeks had gone by. She'd almost started to believe she imagined the whole, crazy thing.

But now he wanted to be alone with her. Wanted to talk to her. Her blood pumped harder. Worst-case scenario, he wanted to fire her. Best-case scenario?

She chewed her lip.

"Annie, darling, could you bring more Chablis?"

She wiped her hands on a towel and headed for the wine cellar.

Three

Sinclair usually preferred to help himself to some toast and coffee, but Annie never knew what guests might want, so she hovered in the kitchen ready to make an omelet or oatmeal. She wondered if Sinclair would come down first and they would have their talk before the others awoke.

To her dismay, Vicki was the first down the stairs, yawning, her sleek black hair knotted into a casual but elegant twist and her taut body showcased in skimpy capris and a cutoff T-shirt. "Morning, Annie. Is this where you ask me if I want breakfast?"

"You're way ahead of me. What can I get you?" Annoying guests weren't unusual. She managed a cheerful smile.

"Do you have any grapefruit?"

"I made a fruit salad of cantaloupe, grapes, honeydew and pineapple, but no grapefruit, I'm afraid. Would you like me to get you some?" Probably she was on some crackpot diet eating twenty-seven grapefruits a day and nothing else. She had that kind of body.

"God, no. Your fruit salad sounds fab. I'd kill for some scrambled eggs and bacon to go with it, if that's a possibility. Any sign of Sinclair?"

Annie blinked. "Not so far."

"Probably snuck out early to avoid us." Vicki shot her a conspiratorial smile. "Not much of a people person, is he?"

Annie glanced up the stairs. Had Sinclair really left the house already? He did sometimes slip away right at dawn. She wasn't sure where he went but he often came back wet, so possibly the beach. He didn't do that when guests were staying, though.

She didn't answer Vicki's question. He seemed very good with people from what she could see. He wouldn't have a successful investment company if he wasn't a people person. "Do you like your bacon well-done?"

"That would be perfect." Vicki wandered into the dining room and picked up the *New York Times*.

Annie headed for the kitchen. People like Vicki gave orders effortlessly. She'd been brought up that way. It was her own job to make sure those orders were carried out without a moment's hesitation, even if she had to run out and wrestle down a pig to make the bacon.

Happily she was well prepared and kept the freshest local bacon on hand. Three rashers were sizzling on the stove and the eggs bubbling in a pan when the kitchen door swung open. Annie nearly jumped out of her skin, expecting to see Sinclair's imposing form and stern gaze.

A smile settled across Vicki's shapely mouth. "Goodness, you are jumpy. Expecting someone else?"

"No." Annie answered too fast. She whisked the bacon and eggs onto a plate, hoping her red face would be attributed to the heat from the stove.

Vicki lounged in the doorway, watching her. "Sinclair is a dark horse."

Annie burned to disagree, or at least ask why she would say such a thing, but her gut told her that would be playing into some plan of Vicki's. "Will you take it in the dining room?"

"I'll take it from you right here." She thrust out her hands and took the fork and knife from Annie. "And thank you very much for making this. It looks yummy." She flashed another oh-so-charming smile.

Annie let out a hard breath when the door closed behind Vicki. What did she mean by that comment? Did she suspect something between herself and Sinclair? Sweat had broken out on her forehead and she pushed a few strands of hair off it. Surely she hadn't given anything away?

Katherine came down around 10:00 a.m. and ate a few bites of her custom-made muesli. "Has my son already abandoned us?"

"I'm not sure. I haven't seen him all morning." Annie refilled her juice. How had Sinclair managed to slip away? She'd been up since before first light. He must be very determined to avoid her. That didn't bode well for their planned talk.

"I'm dying to head up to the attic, though I have to take it slow. The doctor says I'm not allowed to stand up for more than thirty minutes at a time." She shook her head, and her elegant blond bob swung. "I don't know how you're supposed to do anything when you have to sit down every thirty minutes, but he is the top man in his field and I promised Sinclair I'd follow his instructions slavishly."

"How are you feeling?"

"Weak." She laughed a little. "I poop out easily. I'm supposed to eat all kinds of super foods to boost my energy but I don't have any appetite, either. I might try acupuncture. A friend of mine swears by it."

Annie ventured into the conversation. "My sister tried it to give up smoking and it didn't work. I blame my sister, though, not the acupuncturist. I think she was more determined to prove him wrong than she was to quit."

Katherine's warm smile lit up the room. "I'm determined to get well. I have far too much to live for. I haven't even met my first grandchild yet."

Juice sloshed in the jug as Annie's hand jerked. Sinclair was Katherine Drummond's only child so obviously her fondest dreams lay in his next marriage. A prospect that made Annie's muscles limp with dismay. "That is something to look forward to."

"What about you, Annie? Is there anyone in your life?" A blond brow lifted.

Annie froze. Did she also suspect something between her and Sinclair?

"You seem to live here so quietly and I worry that we've cut you off from civilization. Maybe you should try one of those online dating services."

Annie's heart sank a little when she realized it hadn't even crossed Katherine's mind that she and Sinclair might be involved. "I'm quite happy. One day my prince will come." She smiled and hoped it looked convincing.

"These days it doesn't pay to wait around for princes to show up. Better to go out and find one yourself before all the good ones get snatched up."

Sinclair's been snatched up twice, but he's still available. She did not voice her thoughts. And really, was a man who'd been divorced twice such a good prospect? She suppressed a sigh. "I don't have time for dating. I'm planning to take an evening course at the local college."

"Really?" Katherine's eyes widened.

Annie regretted her words. The plan was still half-formed in her mind and now her employer would probably worry about her slacking off in her duties. Why had she said it? Was she so afraid of seeming like a pathetic spinster who'd be polishing silver for the rest of her life?

"Nothing very demanding. I was thinking of learning a little about business." She shrugged her shoulders apologetically. Probably better not to tell Katherine about her dream of opening a shop one day.

"I think that's wonderful, Annie. If there's anything at all I can do to help, a reference to get you into the program, or something like that. I'm sure Sinclair will be thrilled."

She doubted Sinclair would feel such strong emotion on the topic. Though he might be happy to hear she was trying to broaden her employment prospects. He'd hardly want her hanging around in his house for years after they'd had that…accident.

That's what it felt like. A sudden car wreck. Or maybe just a fender bender. Either way it had left her bruised and dented and unsure of her previously planned route.

"Thanks, can I get you some more toast?"

"No, thanks. I'd like to head up to the attic, if you're ready."

They spent the day rifling through the boxes and crates of old possessions. The space grew hotter as the day went on. Vicki was surprisingly quiet, examining objects with a studious eye, as if making mental notes about them. They found several pieces of eighteenth-century scrimshaw and a carefully packed box with two old Chinese vases, but most of the stuff was obviously worthless—boxes of celluloid shirt collars and scrofulous-looking moleskin hats. By late afternoon they were winding down their search. "I think it's time for a glass of iced tea," Katherine said, getting up from the folding chair Annie had brought up for her.

"You go ahead, I'll be down in a minute." Vicki's nose was deep in a black trunk.

"Something interesting in there?" Katherine fanned herself with a slim hand.

"Not sure yet. I'll let you know if I find anything good."

"Let's go down, Annie." Annie cast a backward glance at Vicki. It went against all her instincts to leave her here among the family treasures. "If you'll just give me a hand down the stairs."

With no choice but to help Katherine, Annie headed back into the house and spent the next hour making scones and spreading cream and jam on them, while listening for every slight hint that Sinclair's car might be pulling back into the driveway.

Katherine was nodding off in a shaded armchair, and Vicki engrossed in texting on her phone, when she heard the purr of that familiar engine. Her heart immediately kicked into overdrive. She hurried into the kitchen so she didn't have to watch him kiss Vicki warmly on the cheek. If he wanted to see her, he knew where to find her. She cursed herself for checking her reflection in the polished side of a stainless-steel pot and smoothing her hair back into its bun.

Heavy footfalls on the wood stairs sounded his ascent to his bedroom. She heaved a sigh of relief mingled with disappointment. Obviously he wasn't burning with a desire to see her. She could easily go up there on the pretext of bringing fresh towels or collecting his laundry. In fact, on a normal weekend, she'd probably do just that.

But nothing would ever be normal again.

Softer footfalls on the stairs suggested Vicki heading up, too. Maybe she was going to throw her arms around Sinclair and beg him to tell her all about his sailing adventures.

Annie cursed herself for caring. Sinclair was never hers to be possessive about, not for a single instant. If she didn't want to feel this way, she should never have let him kiss her. If only she could turn the clock back to that moment of madness when his lips hovered just in front of hers.

"He is one of the most insightful portraitists working today, but if you're sure..." Vicki's voice carried along the upstairs hallway later that afternoon. "Katherine, Sin doesn't want to come with us. We're on our own."

"I keep telling him he should pay more attention to art, for its investment potential as well as its beauty, but he won't listen. What time does it open?"

Annie listened to them plan their stroll through the village to the art opening and mentally calculated how long she'd be alone with Sinclair. Certainly long enough to talk. Probably long enough to get into a lot of trouble, too, but she had no intention of doing that again.

She prepped for dinner while the women primped themselves. Katherine was immaculate as usual, her golden hair cupping her cheekbones, dressed in a sleek pantsuit with a bold jade necklace. Vicki looked like she'd just climbed out of bed looking like a goddess, an effect that must take considerable effort. A diaphanous dress clung to her slender form, revealing long, graceful legs that ended in pointy ankle boots.

Annie resisted the urge to look down at herself. She was not in competition with these women. She was not even on the same playing field as them, and no one expected her to be. But then, why did her usual "uniform" of preppy classics feel dowdy and frumpier than ever?

She hid in the kitchen after the door closed behind them. If Sinclair wanted to talk to her he could come find her. And he did.

"I didn't hear you," she stammered, when she saw him standing, tall and serious, in the narrow doorway. The old colonial kitchen had been remodeled with the most extravagant chefs' appliances, but that didn't change the low ceiling and old-fashioned proportions that made Sinclair look like a giant, standing next to the hand-carved spice racks.

His hair was wet, slicked back but with a long tendril falling over his forehead. He wore a pale gray polo shirt and well-worn khakis, and she noticed with a start that his feet were bare. How could he manage to look so elegant and breathtakingly handsome in such casual clothing?

"Listen, Annie…"

Like she had any choice?

"About the other day." He frowned. "I don't know how to explain—"

"Me either," she cut in. "It was very unexpected."

He looked relieved. Somehow that hurt. Still, at least he wasn't trying to act as if nothing happened.

"I think we should both forget that it ever happened."

His mocking echo of her thoughts cut her to the quick. "Of course." The words flew from her mouth, a desperate attempt to save face.

He could have left right then, the pact between them safely sealed, but he didn't. He stood in the doorway, blocking her view of the hallway and—now that she thought of it—her only escape route. "You're a nice girl, Annie."

Oh no, here it came. The "don't be too hurt that I'm not at all interested in you, some other schlub will be" speech. If only she could run from the room and spare herself his pity.

"You're nice, too." She cringed. It sounded like something a preschooler would come up with. No wonder he had no enduring interest in her—she sounded like someone who had the intellect of a turnip.

"Not really." He rubbed at his chest with a tense hand, and she could remember the thick, taut muscle hidden beneath his gray shirt. She'd rested her cheek on his chest and sighed with sheer pleasure. Now his dark eyes looked pained.

He was probably thinking of his ex-wives. The last one had said all kinds of nasty things about him in the press after she realized she hadn't been married long enough to get alimony. "I know you didn't want to... do that." She couldn't even say it. What had they done? It wasn't "making love" or "sleeping together." Having sex. Pretty simple, really, but she still couldn't voice the words. "I know you didn't plan it and that you regret it." She swallowed. What had possibly been the most perfectly blissful hour of her life was an embarrassing footnote in his.

"Exactly."

His words sank through her like a stone. Why could she not shake the pathetic hope that all those kisses and so much passion had meant something to him? It seemed so strange that his breathless moans could be nothing more than a gut physical reaction.

"I don't know what came over me, either." *Except for the fact that I've adored you from afar for far too long.* "But I'll make sure not to try one of those dresses on again." She managed a shaky smile.

One side of Sinclair's mouth lifted, revealing a devastating dimple. "You looked breathtaking in that dress, Annie."

The sound of her name coming from his mouth, right after the compliment, made her heart jump.

"Oh, I think it was the dress that looked breathtaking. They're all so beautifully made. I haven't looked at them since I hung them in the closet but they don't seem to have ever been worn."

"Except that one, now."

"And that wasn't worn for long." She let out a breath. Being in such close quarters with Sinclair played havoc with her sanity. She could smell the familiar scent of that old-fashioned soap he used. She had a close-up view of the lines at the corners of his eyes, which showed how often he smiled, despite all rumors to the contrary. "Maybe there's a reason those clothes ended up in a trunk in the attic and were never worn."

"A curse?" He lifted a dark brow. Humor danced in his eyes. She could tell he didn't believe a word of the superstitions that so excited his mom.

"A spell, perhaps." She played along. "To turn even a sensible woman into a wanton."

"That was a very effective spell." His eyes darkened and held her gaze for a moment until her breath was coming in tiny gasps. "Not that you were a wanton, of course, but…"

"I think we both know what you meant." She shoved a lock off her forehead. She was sweating. If only he knew that the slightest touch from him might accidentally turn her into a wanton at a moment's notice.

Had she imagined it, or did he just sneak a glance at her body? Her breasts tingled slightly under her yellow shirt, and her thighs trembled beneath her khakis. She could almost swear his dark gaze had swept over them and right back up to her face.

But she had no proof and right now that seemed like idle fantasy. Or maybe he was wondering what the heck came over him to find himself in a compromising position with such a frump. He was hardly the type to risk legal trouble with an employee for a quick roll in the hay. The whole incident was truly bizarre.

And totally unforgettable.

Great. Now she just had to spend the rest of her life comparing other men to Sinclair Drummond.

He walked across the kitchen and took a glass from one of the cabinets. She should have asked him if he wanted something, but it was too late now. His biceps flexed, tightening the cuff of his polo shirt as he reached to close the cabinet. She watched the muscles of his back extend and contract beneath the soft fabric, which pulled slightly from the top of his khakis. Just enough for her to remember sliding her fingers into his waistband and...

She turned and headed for the dishwasher. This line of thought was not at all productive. "Can I get you some iced tea?"

"No, thanks, Annie. I'll help myself to some water." He pushed the glass into the dispenser on the front of the fridge.

She'd have to find another job. This was way too awkward. How was she supposed to wait hand and foot on a man while remembering how his body felt pressed against hers?

There was no way she'd find a job that paid as well as this one, where she'd get to live—free of charge—in a beautiful house near the beach and be her own boss 95 percent of the time. She didn't have a college degree. She hadn't even finished high school properly. This job had allowed her to pile up savings in the bank, and she was about to fulfill her dream of going to college right nearby. If she left she'd probably eat into her savings subsidizing her "Would you like fries with that?" job.

Sinclair's Adam's apple moved as he drained his glass of water. How awkward that they were in the same room, not talking at all. Then again, that wouldn't have been at all strange until two weeks ago. Sinclair wasn't the chatty type, and neither was she. They were both the kind of people who enjoyed listening to the sounds of a spring evening, or just letting thoughts glide through their heads.

Or at least she presumed that's what he was doing. Maybe it was all in her imagination. She was so different than the rest of her family, who seemed hell-bent on filling every moment with talk, music or the sound of the television. Maybe other people were quiet for different reasons.

"My mom wants to stay here for the rest of the summer." A tiny line appeared between his brows as he said it. "And I do think it's the best thing for her. The fresh air will do her good, and she can rest with you to take care of things."

"That's great." Her heart was sinking. Much as she liked Katherine Drummond, all she wanted right now was to be alone to lick her wounds. The prospect of having to be "on" all the time seemed unbearable. And maybe this was Sinclair's way of saying, *Don't quit until the summer's over. My ailing mom needs you.*

"Vicki will be here to keep her company, so you won't have to feel obliged to entertain her."

Annie flinched, accidentally knocking against a canister of sugar. Could this get any worse? Sinclair obviously knew this was all unwelcome news. He shoved his hand through his hair again, ruffling it. "And Mom's convinced me to work from here for the next couple of weeks at least. She thinks I'm working too hard." His dark gaze held hers for a second.

"Great." The word sounded empty and insincere.

"You and I are both sensible adults." His dark eyes fixed on hers. Was he trying to convince her? "I'm sure we can move beyond what happened."

"Of course." She didn't want him to know how much

that afternoon had meant to her. He must never know. It was hard to look at him. Even the world-weary aspect of his face only added to his charm, his gaze hooded and guarded. She wasn't sure he wanted any woman, least of all her. "I'll be the soul of discretion."

The furrow in his brow deepened for a second. "I knew I could count on you, Annie." The sound of her own name sent a jolt of pain to her heart. Hearing it on his lips made her yearn for when he'd breathed it in passion. It seemed so...intimate. She could never say *Sinclair* so boldly and often.

But that was the problem, wasn't it? They were from completely different social strata. In the twenty-first century that shouldn't matter, but it did. She might have been able to climb to a different level herself if she'd managed to go to college and start a successful career, like his. She could have been an executive by now, rubbing shoulders with him in a New York City boardroom.

But that wasn't how things had worked out. She was destined to rub shoulders with him while wielding a sponge in his kitchen.

She wished he would leave. This was so awkward. He kept...looking at her. But it was his kitchen and she was his employee. He could stand there and look pityingly on her all day if he wanted. And now she couldn't even start combing the classifieds. She could hardly leave his mother in the lurch while she was still so weak.

"I'm heading out for a walk." Still he hovered in the kitchen, his large, masculine presence filling the room.

"Okay." As if her opinion mattered.

He hesitated again, brow furrowed, and pierced her soul one more time with that intense brown gaze before he turned and left.

She sank against the countertop as the sound of his footsteps echoed down the hallway. How was she going to survive this summer? The worst part was that she kept feeling something that he wasn't saying. Something odd and unsettling in the way he looked at her. Like some of the madness still lingered inside him the way it did inside her.

But that hardly mattered if he intended for them to forget that magical afternoon ever happened. She'd just have to get through it one day at a time. Starting with tonight's dinner.

Four

Sinclair stayed in his room as long as possible, reading research one of his staff had compiled on a gold-mining company in Uruguay. He'd much rather be at work than "relaxing" here with his mom organizing things for him to do every minute of the day. Today's festivities included a croquet party she'd arranged, and he was expected to put in an appearance and actually wield a mallet. If she hadn't come so close to death... He let out a long breath, then closed his laptop and swung his feet off the bed.

"Sinclair, is that you?" His mom's voice came from the corridor. Had she been listening outside, waiting for him to betray signs of life? He shook his head and ran his fingers through his hair. She'd probably arranged for eight to ten attractive single women, dressed in designer croquet attire, to battle each other to win his heart.

Couldn't any of them tell he didn't have a heart to win?
"I'll be down in a minute."

"Good, dear, because everyone's here."

A glance out the window confirmed that "everyone"
was at least fifteen of Dog Harbor's most well-heeled
citizens. They milled about clutching drinks, stiletto
heels sinking into the smooth lawn. He yawned. His
mother's social occasions made even the most brutal
business negotiations seem like a cakewalk.

And Annie would be there. Not playing croquet,
or batting her eyelashes, but serving the iced tea and
salmon squares. He searched for her among the small
crowd but didn't see her. The resulting wave of disappointment shocked him away from the window and toward the door, tucking in his shirt and smoothing his
hair on the way. Maybe all these people would at least
take his mind off Annie for a while.

Either that or he was losing it for good. Lust. That's
what it was. The curse of mankind, or at least the male
half of the species. Abstinence didn't really work for
men; they just ended up doing something crazier and
more stupid than if they'd been in a normal relationship.

Shame he wasn't capable of a normal relationship.
Two failed marriages didn't leave too much doubt about
that.

He descended the stairs and went out to the garden. Voices called out, "Sinclair, how lovely to see you!
It's been such a long time." Scented kisses covered his
cheeks and he was forced to make fluff conversation
about how his business was doing. Happily, neither of
his ex-wives was there, but several of their close friends

were. No doubt his mother considered them potential future wives. She was nothing if not determined.

"Would you like a glass of white wine?" Annie's soft voice made him whip around.

"Iced tea would be fine, thanks." The words sounded so inadequate, so laughable, after what had happened between them. A pang of regret stabbed him as she moved silently away to get his drink. He'd made things so awkward with a lovely woman who deserved to be treated with respect, not stripped naked by a man who couldn't control his basest urges.

"You're up first, Sinclair." His mother, beaming and looking happier and healthier than he'd seen her in ages, thrust a mallet into his hand. She loved parties and was never happier than when entertaining. Of course she wasn't a true Drummond. She'd married into the family, or she might have shared the taste for solitude that so annoyed her in his father and himself. None of the other Drummonds she'd tried to contact about the cup had bothered to respond. He wouldn't have either if she wasn't his own mother.

Annie returned with his drink. "Oh, you're playing now. Maybe I'd better hold on to it for you." Her lashes were a dark gold color that turned darker at the root near her pale blue eyes. Her hand hovered, waiting to see if he'd take the drink. His groin tightened and heated as a memory flashed over him—of the lush, curvy body hidden beneath her loose-fitting clothes.

"I'll take it now." He grabbed the glass rather roughly, afraid he'd somehow betray the fever of arousal that suddenly gripped him. All he needed was her lingering somewhere nearby, drink in hand, while he attempted to tap a wooden ball around the lawn.

"We haven't seen you out here in ages, Sinclair. If your family hadn't owned the place since biblical times I'd worry you were going to sell." A sleek brunette he recognized from the yacht club held her drink up near her ear as a smile hovered around her glossy lips.

"Couldn't do that. The ancestors would rise up and haunt me."

"We're doing teams." His mother rushed over. "Sinclair, why don't you team up with Lally." She gestured toward the brunette, who murmured that she'd love to.

Sinclair's heart sank. Why couldn't people leave him alone? Now Lally would be offended if he didn't flirt with her vigorously enough, and again when he failed to ask her out. Or, if he did ask her out from a sense of duty, she'd be upset when he didn't want to sleep with her. Maybe he should sleep with her right here and get it over with.

His flesh recoiled from the possibility. "Sure. Why don't you start?" He handed his partner the mallet, and she handed him her drink to hold. It looked like Annie's famous Long Island iced tea, a shot of every white liquor plus a splash of Coke for color. It tasted deceptively sweet and was utterly lethal. He contemplated downing it in one gulp.

"Oh, no, we're short a hand." His mom rushed around, stabbing in the air with her finger as she counted the assembled guests. "Philip canceled at the last minute with a toothache."

Lucky Philip. No doubt he'd found something better to do than be clawed over by single girls with ticking biological clocks.

"How's your hedge fund doing in this market?" The brunette, Lally, attempted to look interested. He launched into his standard dinner-party-conversation reply, leaving the rest of his mind free to wonder what about her made his mom see her as third-wife material. She was pretty, mid-twenties, slim as a kebab prong. All things his mom found essential. Personally he preferred a woman with some curves to hold on to, but apparently that wasn't fashionable anymore. Her teeth looked like Chiclets, or maybe that was an effect of her ultrawide smile and overglossed lips.

"Wow, that's so cool. It must be wonderful to be good with numbers."

His mom flapped toward him. "Darling, have you seen Annie? We need her to make up the last team."

Sinclair stiffened. "She can't have gone far." She was probably hiding in the pantry, trying to avoid getting roped into this charade. Since when did anyone over ten play croquet, anyway? "She's probably busy."

"Nonsense. I had everything catered and people can help themselves to drinks. I'll go find her."

Sinclair swallowed and returned his attention to Lally, who'd moved so close he was in danger of being suffocated by her expensive scent. He resisted the urge to recoil. "What do you do?" This was usually a good question to keep someone talking for a while.

She threw her head back slightly. "It's rather a revolutionary idea, actually." She looked about, as if worried someone might overhear and steal it, but with a big smile like she was hoping they would. "I host Botox parties. You know, where people come and have their cares smoothed away."

Genuine horror provoked Sinclair's curiosity. "You mean where people come and have a neurotoxin injected into their face?"

She laughed. "It's absolutely harmless in small doses, otherwise I'd be dead, wouldn't I?"

Sinclair blinked. "You've used Botox? You can't be a day over twenty-five."

She winked conspiratorially. "Twenty-nine, but don't tell a soul. I'm living proof that the product works." He couldn't resist staring at her forehead, which was smooth as the backside of his titanium laptop. "Still think it's crazy?"

"Absolutely." He had a violent urge to get as far away from Lally as possible, but politeness demanded that he survive this round of croquet first.

"You should invest. I'm going to be taking the company public some time next year. Of course, my main goal is to get bought out by a…" She rambled on, but his attention shifted to the sudden appearance of Annie. His mom had hooked her arm around Annie's and pulled her onto the lawn. Annie looked rather startled and, he noted with alarm, teary-eyed. Was she okay? Her nose was red as if she'd been crying.

"You don't need to know the rules. Just follow along. Your team will go last so you'll have plenty of time to figure it out, and Dwight will be happy to explain anything you miss, won't you, Dwight?" The tall, sandy-haired male with whom Sinclair had shared a long-ago sailing holiday agreed effusively. Jealousy kicked Sinclair in the gut.

"Are you okay?" He couldn't help asking her.

Annie looked up with a start. "Sure, I'm fine." She spoke quickly, her voice rather high. "It's allergies. They're terrible at this time of year."

He frowned. He didn't remember her having allergies, but no doubt that was just one of the many things he didn't know about her.

"Sinclair, we're up first." The feel of soft fingers on his back made him flinch. Lally tugged him up to the start. "You should watch so you see where the ball goes." Her vigorous tap sent the ball flying through the first hoop and raised a smatter of applause from the gathered crowd. Lally turned to him beaming, which, he noticed, had no effect on any other part of her face than her mouth. He handed her drink back to her, partly to ease the temptation of knocking it back to dull the pain of being there.

He snuck a glance over her shoulder at Annie. Her eyes had dried and she was engaged in conversation with Dwight about something very entertaining, at least judging from the way she kept laughing. His muscles tightened. What could Dwight be saying that was so funny? He didn't remember him being such a wit. He strained to hear their conversation, but couldn't make out a word of it over a nearby damsel bleating about her new vacation villa in Saint Lucia.

Annie's nose had a light sprinkling of freckles, and a sweet way of wrinkling as she talked. She didn't throw her chin and limbs around to punctuate her conversation the way the ambitious Lally was currently doing. He managed to nod in pretend interest to her conversational foray about yachting in the Caribbean. But all the while he was sneaking glances at Annie. He was glad her usual attire hid her hourglass figure, with its high, full breasts and slim waist. He could still feel the curve of her shapely backside against his hand.

"What did I do with my drink?" he asked, cutting Lally short.

"I don't know. Where's that girl who was passing them out?" She looked behind her. "Oh, there she is. Sinclair needs a drink!"

Sinclair stiffened as Annie looked his way. Her eyebrow lifted slightly. "Of course. Wine, or something stronger?"

He fought the urge to laugh. She could see right through him. "No, no. I'm fine."

"But you just said—" Lally's smooth face almost blocked his view of Annie.

"I said, I'm fine. If I need something I'll get it myself." His curt response rather startled both women. He attempted to lighten up. "I can't believe you're worrying about drinks during this cutthroat game of croquet. Your attention should be fixed entirely on the fate of our balls."

Dwight guffawed. "Easy for you to say, Sin. Some of us are still holding our balls." He winked at Annie, and again Sinclair felt a hot flash of unfamiliar emotion.

"Don't be so crude, Dwight." Vicki materialized beside him. "You'll shock Sinclair. He's a man of old-fashioned tastes and sensibilities."

She was right, of course. Though he couldn't understand why his mother had invited Vicki for what was apparently going to be an extended stay. He hadn't seen her more than in passing for years, and his mom could hardly think Vicki was going to be his next wife. Then again, his mom could get strange ideas.

"My son is a gentleman of the old style." His mom materialized next to him. Was this some kind of staged sketch where everyone knew their lines except him? "I think we all have a lot to learn from him."

He snuck another glance at Annie. She was looking

down at her croquet mallet like she wished she was anywhere but here. The feeling was mutual. The only safe course of action was to wrap this hellish game up as soon as possible. "My turn, I believe." Having a strategic nature, he'd been taking mental notes while his opponents tapped their balls ineffectually around the course. He sliced his through the hoop at an angle, taking out two other balls on the way, then drove it hard through the next two hoops without blinking. He would have happily launched it all the way to the home post but that wouldn't be sporting, so he pretended to miss and set his ball up to knock his opponents' flying.

"I am glad I'm on your team, Sinclair." Lally's un-lined face glowed. "You're quite ruthless."

If only he was ruthless enough to tell his mom to leave him in peace and stop trying to enhance his social life. She probably wouldn't leave him alone until he married again, now she'd got the future of the Drummond dynasty on her mind. On the one hand, he actually liked the idea of having children. They'd be a lot more fun to play croquet with than this crowd. The marriage part, on the other hand, he wasn't up for at all. Women changed once you put that ring on their finger.

"Hey, Sinclair, do you remember me?" A svelte redhead in a green dress sauntered over, mallet in one hand and drink in the other.

"Of course, Mindy."

"I hear Diana's in Greece for the summer."

Why did people think he'd want to know what his ex-wife was doing? "I imagine that will be good for the Greek economy."

Mindy laughed. "You're such a card, Sinclair. And not at all bitter! I love that in a man."

"I'm glad to see everyone getting along so well." His mom walked among them, wreathed in smiles and carrying a tray of pastries. "Such a lovely way to spend a summer afternoon."

"Let me pass those around." Annie leaped forward and tried to wrest the pastries from his mom's hand.

"I wouldn't dream of it." His mom waved her away. "You're a member of our party now and have a far more important role to play."

Annie glanced nervously at him. As their eyes met, a jolt of raw and unsettling energy flashed between them. He looked away sharply. Why Annie? Why did he have to share steamy, hungry and unfettered sex in the arms of the one woman he'd previously enjoyed an utterly uncomplicated relationship with?

Obviously the gossips were right and he was simply impossible.

Emotionally exhausted from the effort of not looking at Sinclair, while attempting to make polite small talk and to participate in a game she'd never played before, Annie washed and rinsed the serving platters when all she wanted was to crawl into her bed and sob. Earlier, in an uncharacteristic Cinderella moment, she'd become teary-eyed while plating the caterer's canapés and watching all those beautiful women pulling into the driveway, dressed to impress and woo him. She'd been discovered mid-sniffle by Katherine. Now she was going to have to stage a pretense of using antihistamine drops and sneezing over flowers for the rest of the summer.

"What's going on between you and Sinclair?"

She almost had a heart attack when she realized

Vicki was standing behind her. Had she been muttering to herself? Did she say something about Sinclair?

"Nothing."

"Goodness, no need to bite my head off." Vicki reached for a slightly shriveled cheese puff from a nearby plate that had not yet been cleared. "I can see I've hit a nerve."

"I don't know what you're talking about," she lied.

"Hmm. The color rushing to your cheeks contradicts your words. Don't tell me you don't find him attractive, because I wouldn't believe you. I think he's gorgeous." She ate the cheese puff and reached for another. "Handsome and rich. What more could a woman want?"

"Are you asking me a question, or just thinking aloud?" Letting Vicki think she was a mousy pushover didn't feel like a good idea.

Vicki laughed, tossing back her silky black mane. "Thinking aloud, I suppose. Do you think I'd look good in a wedding picture next to him?" She lifted a slender brow. It was hard to tell if she was joking or not.

The image of her haughty, delicate features next to Sinclair's sent a fist of hurt to Annie's heart. "You'd make a very attractive couple," she said truthfully.

"Shame that isn't enough, really, is it?" Vicki moved closer and pulled a piece of celery from another platter. Annie wished she could physically shove her out of the kitchen. "Life would be so much easier if you only had to look good together."

"I suspect Sinclair would agree." She knew he'd been devastated by the failure of his second marriage. Partly from snippets of conversations she'd overheard, but also by a dramatic shift in his demeanor after his wife left him.

"What happened between him and Diana?"

"I really don't know."

"Come on, you're in the same house."

"Diana didn't like Dog Harbor. Too dull. They hardly ever came after they got married." Though he'd come here a lot afterward, probably to lick his wounds in peace. "I don't know what they got up to elsewhere."

"Rather like watching only one story thread on a soap opera." Vicki leaned one hip against the kitchen counter and crossed her arms. She wore a dress of crinkly white parachute fabric that revealed a lot of slender, barely tanned leg. "I bet you wish you could TiVo the rest of the episodes sometimes."

"I have plenty of other things to keep me busy." Annie scrubbed at a stubborn grease spot. "What they did was none of my business."

"I'm not so sure." Vicki regarded her silently for a moment. "I'd think that since it's your job to keep Sinclair happy, what he's up to is your business."

Annie threw down her sponge. "My job is to keep the house clean and make sure there's milk in the fridge when he shows up." Her voice rose, along with frustration and humiliation at being forced to endure Vicki's inquisition. If they were on neutral territory she could tell her to get lost, or simply walk away. But here, Vicki was a guest of her employer, so she couldn't.

"Now, now, don't burst a blood vessel." Vicki's eyes were brightening, if anything. "I suspect there's a lot more to you behind that placid smile." She studied Annie's face for a moment, as Annie's blood pressure rose. "I've seen Sinclair looking at you, too."

"Why wouldn't he? I'm his employee." This was almost unbearable. She was lying with one side of her brain, while the other madly considered Vicki's bold statements. Was Sinclair really looking at her differently? And how would Vicki know? She hadn't seen him for years. Probably she was just trying to wind her up. "It's hard to wash these dishes with you distracting me."

"So leave them. They're not going anywhere."

"I can't. I have to get dinner ready soon and they'll be in the way."

Vicki tilted her head to the side. "It can't be easy slaving away in the kitchen while everyone else reclines on the patio and sips champagne. I think it would drive me half-mad."

"It's my job. We all have one."

"Do we?"

"Sinclair works very hard at his business."

Vicki's eyebrow shot up again. "You are loyal. And I'm sure you're right. In fact, sometimes I wonder if he'd ever do anything else unless someone forced him into it."

"Is it wrong to enjoy your work?"

"I think it's ideal." Vicki frowned.

"Do you work at an auction house?" Annie couldn't resist asking. She'd been wondering if Vicki had a real job.

"Between you, me and this wilted stalk of celery, I'm between gigs right now." She took a bite of the celery.

"I suppose you're independently wealthy." She rinsed the dish and put it in the rack.

"Something like that." Vicki shot her a fake smile. "Gotta dash. It's been interesting chatting with you." Annie felt herself relaxing as Vicki moved toward the door with her characteristic floaty walk. "And I still think there's something going on between you and Sinclair."

The next morning Katherine asked Annie to help her search the attic. Mercifully, Sinclair was out playing golf with a business prospect, but unfortunately Vicki was there, her violet eyes seeming to peer below the surface of every human interaction.

"This set of hunting knives is probably worth something." Vicki held one of the tarnished blades up to the light. She jotted something in a little notebook. "I could find a home for it if you like."

Annie frowned. She'd noticed Vicki taking an interest in many of the items. She'd filled quite a few pages with notes.

"That's probably a good idea. What would we do with them anyway?"

"They're just moldering away up here."

"They are part of the Drummond family history." Annie felt called upon to suggest that Sinclair might want them someday. Of course it wasn't her place to say that explicitly.

"True." Katherine looked thoughtfully at an odd contraption of leather and woven rope. "Though perhaps the Drummonds need to shed some of this unhelpful baggage in order to make room for wonderful new things. That's what my friend Claire says. She's mad about feng shui."

"I couldn't agree more." Vicki made another note in her book. "Sometimes an object will sit in one place for a hundred years, doing nothing but collect dust, when in another person's hands it could enjoy full and active use."

Annie tried to picture some of these objects taking on new lives. Did anyone really have a use for old celluloid shirt collars? Then again, future generations might one day enjoy seeing the crazy things their ancestors wore. "I think Sinclair's children might have fun going through these things one day."

Katherine looked up as if shot. She paused a moment, then nodded. "You're absolutely right, of course, Annie. We'll put everything back where we found it."

Annie couldn't resist a glance at Vicki, who glared at her for a split second, then assumed a forced smile.

She enjoyed a brief flash of pride at defending Sinclair's inheritance. "Did you hear back from the other branches of the family?" She knew Katherine had sent them both letters.

"Not a word. I phoned about a week after sending the letters. I left a message with some elderly Scottish person at the family estate in the Highlands, but no one has called back. For the Florida branch, I left a message on some robotic voice mail system so I don't even know if anyone heard it. Exasperating, really. It would be pointless finding one part of the cup if we can't convince them to produce the others."

"Do they even know about the cup?" Annie sorted through some mismatched plates.

"They do now, if they got my letters. I know there's bad blood between the branches of the family, but it's time to put that behind us. Sinclair's father is gone, and so are most of the Drummonds of his generation. Which is proof enough that the family needs to change its luck. The ones in charge now are all Sinclair's age, or close, and have no reason to feel enmity toward each other. Young people these days don't carry centuries-old grudges for no reason."

"Or do they?" Vicki asked enigmatically.

"Sinclair doesn't." Katherine shook out a brocaded jacket. "Of course, the flipside is that he shows no interest whatsoever in the family or its history." She sighed and let the jacket fall in her lap. "Including the pressing need to produce the next generation."

Annie cringed. If she wasn't on birth control she might have had the next generation of Drummonds growing inside her right now. They certainly hadn't stopped to chat about contraception in their rush to tear each other's clothes off.

"There's still plenty of time." Vicki looked up from making notes on a set of spoons. "He's young."

"I know, but I'm not. I want to enjoy my grandchildren while I'm healthy and energetic enough to have fun with them."

Annie wanted to laugh. Katherine Drummond barely looked forty-five. Though that was probably due to the art of a number of fine surgeons and dermatologists. She was probably somewhere in her late fifties. Hardly old, however you looked at it.

"Sinclair will find the right woman eventually." Vicki peered into a small wooden chest.

"Will he? I'm not so sure. He found the first two by himself and I think it's time I took over. He needs women who aren't so driven by personal ambition. Sinclair doesn't want to set the world on fire or fly around in private jets every weekend. He needs someone quiet and simple."

Annie's soul nodded in agreement. Maybe she really was perfect for Sinclair, and they'd all realize it if she only waited patiently.

Vicki laughed. "I'm not sure many women want to be described that way. I know I wouldn't."

"I don't mean simple-minded, just someone without complex ulterior motives. Sinclair is a simple man, brilliant—"

"And gorgeous...."

"But simple." Katherine and Vicki said it together, then laughed. Annie had a feeling Sinclair would hate being discussed in this trivializing fashion. Didn't they care if he loved the woman?

"So I take it this means I'm not supposed to sink my own claws into him." Vicki lifted a cloudy etched-glass trophy and peered at it. Or pretended to.

Katherine shrugged. "For all I know, you're the breath of fresh air he needs. At least you've always been a straight shooter and everyone knows where they stand with you."

"Some would say that's my least attractive feature."

"Only if you don't want to hear the truth." Katherine smiled.

Annie's mind raced. Had Vicki been telling the truth about how Sinclair looked at her? Maybe he really was still attracted to her. Or perhaps even had deeper feelings.

Heat rushed inside her and she walked to the far end of the attic to bury herself in shadows. If these women had any idea what was going through her mind—and who knew what powers of perception Vicki possessed beyond those she boasted—they'd be scandalized. As it was, they talked about Sinclair's love life right in front of her as if she didn't exist. It obviously didn't cross

Katherine's mind that her beloved son might have had an affair, no matter how brief, with the woman who served the *brie en croute* and refilled her wineglass.

She let out a quiet sigh.

"He didn't seem to like Lally much, did he?"

"Not at all. I think that shows excellent taste on his part."

"She's from a very good family," said Katherine with conviction.

"Is that important?"

"I think so. Don't you?"

"Not in the least. I've always secretly dreamed of marrying one of the dastardly Drummonds, despite the family's dubious reputation."

"Oh, Vicki. You and Sinclair would make a striking couple."

"So I was telling Annie." Vicki shot a glance at her, where she hid in the shadows. "She completely agreed."

Katherine clapped her hands together and laughed. "Well, then, maybe things are moving in the right direction."

Vicki glanced at Annie again, as if seeking her gaze, but Annie kept herself busy rummaging through a tall chest of drawers. Was Vicki deliberately trying to torment her? Maybe she took pleasure in the fact that she could have Sinclair if she wanted to, and Annie couldn't.

Whoever said life was supposed to be fair? Her grandmother's ominous words rang in her ears. If she wanted to keep her sanity, she needed to forget that wild afternoon of lovemaking ever happened.

If only it were that easy.

Five

Her heart pounded with trepidation as she approached Sinclair. He'd been gone for much of the past week, out sailing, fishing or playing tennis. She might suspect he was trying to avoid someone, if she didn't already know that was true.

But she couldn't hold her tongue any longer.

I'm crazy about you.

No, she wasn't going to say that, though the thought almost drove a manic laugh to her lips. She drew in a deep breath as she opened the door to the sitting room. "Sinclair?"

He was reading alone, in front of the big, carved fireplace. No fire burned, since it was downright hot and the house, being ancient, had no air-conditioning. He looked up from his newspaper. "Hello, Annie."

Her insides melted. Why did he always greet her by name? Did he know that it half killed her to hear her name—boring as it was—fall from his mouth in that deep, warm tone? It would be so much better if he just uttered a curt "What?"

"Um." She pushed a lock of hair behind her ears. Then glanced behind her. She didn't want anyone to overhear what she was about to say. "It's about Vicki. Do you mind if I close the door?"

He frowned slightly, and curiosity appeared in his eyes. "This sounds mysterious." He glanced at the door. She took that as an invitation and quickly shut it.

"She's been up in the attic with your mom and me, looking through all the old stuff." She paused, wondering how to say this next part.

"I know. That's why she's here, ostensibly." He leaned toward her slightly, and she felt the increased closeness almost like a hug. Which was ridiculous, since she was still several feet away.

"It probably isn't my place to say anything, but I couldn't keep quiet because I know the house and everything in it is important to you."

He regarded her with no expression. Probably thought she was nuts. Maybe it would be better if she didn't say anything. In some ways it was none of her business. On the other hand she was the housekeeper, which, taken literally, could mean she was responsible for keeping the house from being looted. "Vicki's been taking detailed notes on a lot of the items in the attic, and I've seen her researching them on her laptop."

"She's an antique dealer."

"I know. I've also seen her looking at auctions on eBay. I think she might be planning to sell some of the items."

"Perhaps my mom has asked her to. There's way too much junk up there."

She shook her head. "I heard her bring the idea up, and your mom said we should put everything back where we found it, to save it for your children." She didn't mention her own part in helping Katherine to that decision.

"Typical." He shook his head. "Why does everyone have to have children? Would it be such a tragedy if this branch of the Drummonds died out with me? Put it all on eBay. That's what I say." A wry smile played about his lips. "But I do appreciate you worrying about the fate of our old junk. It's very thoughtful."

Was he making fun of her? He certainly didn't seem to care whether Vicki took everything home in her suitcase. Maybe he really didn't want children and everything in the house would end up at an auctioneer one day. "You should have children."

She gasped when she heard her own words on the air. Sinclair sat up slightly in his chair, startled. "I can see you feel strongly about it. May I ask why?" Humor glittered in the depths of his eyes.

She wished she could melt into the Persian carpet. *Because you'd be a great father. Strict, but kind. Because children would bring out the child buried inside you.* "I don't know. It would be a waste, that's all. And your mom would be very disappointed."

"She'll survive. I don't live my life to please other people."

"Don't you want children?" Why did she keep digging herself further into this hole? Sheer burning curiosity drove her to ask.

"I used to, once." He looked up at the window. Then

his brow furrowed. "But I don't intend to be a single father and apparently there isn't a woman alive who can put up with me."

"That's not true." Her heart squeezed. Did he really feel so totally unlovable? "You just haven't met the right person yet." The light played in his dark hair and across his bold cheekbones. If only she could tell him that he had met the right person and she was standing here in front of him.

But he'd told her to forget their magical afternoon ever happened. He wasn't interested in her. He'd lost control for a short while, and now that his sanity was back he wanted nothing from her. Well, other than freshly laundered sheets and homemade dinners.

His brow had furrowed slightly and an odd expression played across his sensual mouth. "Maybe you're right." He looked away sharply. "I don't know."

Tension thickened in the air. Her fault. She'd come in here and started this far-too-personal conversation after accusing one of his old friends of fraud. She'd be lucky if they didn't fire her. "I'd better go make dinner."

"Yes, you'd better." That glint of amusement twinkled in his eyes again. "Before you make any more rash and unsettling statements."

Something hovered between them. Unspoken words. Feelings that weren't supposed to be felt. At least she felt them. Maybe he just wished she'd leave him in peace.

She turned and hurried for the door before she could make things worse.

During dinner, conversation turned to an upcoming dance to be held by a music mogul celebrating his twentieth wedding anniversary.

"We ran into his wife, Jess, at the nursery today." Katherine almost shone with excitement. "She was looking at floral arrangements for the centerpieces. Apparently everyone up this end of Long Island is invited, and when I told her Vicki was staying she insisted that she come with Sinclair. Oh, it will be sensational. I wish I was feeling strong enough to come. I remember the party they gave to celebrate their son's graduation— an entire Russian ballet company performed and there were a hundred black swans swimming on that big lake behind their conservatory. Vicki will need something *fabulous* to wear."

Annie disappeared back into the kitchen, carrying the dishes from the main course of swordfish steaks with spinach sautéed in sesame oil. She did feel a little like Cinderella right now. Everyone would be going to the ball, and it wouldn't even cross their minds that she might be sad about not being invited.

She returned with freshly made peach pie and a jug of thick cream.

"We'll have to go into the city. A trip to Madison Avenue is definitely in order." Katherine looked like she was ready to leap out of her chair and hail a cab right now.

"I'm not so sure." Vicki looked oddly hesitant. "I probably have something I can wear."

"But darling, this is the perfect occasion for a big splurge. I saw this amazing purple dress at Fendi when I was in visiting my doctor. It would look so striking with your complexion."

"Oh, I don't know. Sinclair, are you going to buy yourself a shiny new dinner jacket?"

"God, no." Katherine spoke for him. "He'd wear an-

tiques from his father's closet if I let him. I'll make sure
he looks presentable." She flashed him an indulgent
smile, which he ignored.

"You've given me an idea." Vicki paused, cream jug
in her hand. "Well, maybe it's crazy."

"What?" Katherine leaned forward.

"Those dresses you found up in the attic, before I
arrived. Maybe I could wear one of those."

Annie froze in the doorway where she stood with a
tray of brandy snaps. Her heart crumpled at the thought
of Vicki swanning through the house wearing that
peacock-blue dress that had totally deprived Sinclair
of his sanity.

"What a marvelous idea. If they don't fit we could
always get one altered. But you're so slim you could
wear anything and look good. They're all hanging in
the spare bedroom downstairs, for reasons beyond my
comprehension. There's a blue one in there that's stunning. It looks like Thai silk, with a glorious shimmer."

Annie glanced at Sinclair, who picked up his wineglass and took a gulp of the white wine.

She slunk back into the kitchen. This must be some
kind of lesson in humility. Now she'd have to see Vicki
wearing the dress to a party the way its maker must
have intended. Her donning it, even for a few minutes,
was a foolish mistake that continued to have humiliat-
ing repercussions.

"Let's go look at them now, before dessert." Katherine rose from her chair. "It'll be fun. Annie, do come
with us. You can help us move them somewhere more
sensible."

She wanted to make some excuse about needing to
decant the ice cream but her brain wasn't fast enough.

"Okay." She followed mutely as they walked down the hallway to the spare bedroom with its big walnut wardrobe.

"What a lovely shade of lavender." Katherine pulled a hanger from the rack. A pale, almost snowy, lavender dress billowed on the hanger. The wrinkles from years of packing seemed to have fallen out of it, leaving it ready to wear. Delicate black beading around the neckline and sleeves added a touch of drama. "Who were these made for, I wonder? The quality is so exquisite."

Sinclair stood in the doorway, almost filling the frame. His dark blue polo shirt stretched across his broad chest as he leaned against the doorjamb. He looked indulgently at his mother. "Probably someone who died before she had a chance to wear them. It was a different world back then. People died almost overnight from things that barely warrant a doctor's visit today."

Annie was touched by how much he obviously cared about his mom. He'd all but abandoned his work and thrown himself into keeping her happy and entertained since her illness began. If she didn't already admire Sinclair, she would now.

"You're so right. Still, it might be interesting to find out. I wonder if she was a Drummond by birth, or someone who married into the family." She pulled out a gray-green dress with a dramatic dark red trim. "It was obviously someone rather fashionable."

"I've done some research, actually." Vicki moved forward. "The trunk the dresses were stored in had the maker's name on it, from Lyme, Connecticut."

Annie snuck a glance at Sinclair while everyone listened to Vicki. His eyes looked slightly shadowed, tired—or haunted. How she'd love to get him to relax for a while. He never seemed to be able to relax when there were other people in the house. He was quite a different person on the rare weekends he came out here by himself.

When it was just him and her.

Though of course he didn't think of it like that. He probably thought of it as being there alone, since she served a similar function as the anonymous mailman, or the gardener who pruned the bushes and trimmed the lawn.

"Ran away with the groom! You're joking." Katherine's shriek dragged Annie back to the present. "I didn't think anyone did that outside of mournful ballads. I bet she lived to regret it."

"Well." Vicki rearranged her artfully casual bun. "The man she was supposed to marry, Temperance Drummond, tried to have the groom arrested for theft."

"Of his fiancée?" Sinclair raised a brow.

"Of his horse and cart. The groom was part of her personal staff from Connecticut, but he absconded with the master's soon-to-be lady in the Drummonds' carriage."

"Did they find her?" Katherine looked fascinated.

"Nope. At least there's no record of it that I could find. They disappeared into thin air in 1863 and were never seen again. Or at least not around here." She turned to Sinclair with a raised brow. "What do you think happened to them? Did they travel out west, join a wagon train and get rich in the gold rush in California?"

"Who knows? Maybe they did." Sinclair looked thoughtful. "Though I doubt it."

"What about you, Annie? Do you think they enjoyed decades of happy marriage?"

She shrugged. Vicki's attention was always uncomfortable. She was too much of a loose cannon.

"Do you think people from different social circles can live happily ever after?"

Annie shrank. Worse yet, her gaze darted involuntarily toward Sinclair, and met his. A jolt of energy shocked her. She groped for a response in the hope that no one would see how flustered she was. "I don't see why not. If they have the right things in common."

"I'm not so sure." Sinclair's mother fingered the black trim on the lavender dress. "I think one tends to have more shared interests with someone from one's own circles. Sinclair's father has been gone a long time and I've never had the slightest interest in dating the gardener." She laughed as if the very idea was comical. Which it was. The gardener was a taut and muscular woman of about twenty-five. "Though I do admire her abs when she wears those cutoff tops."

They all laughed. Annie was glad that the moment of tension had been defused. "They're lovely dresses. It's a shame she didn't take them with her."

"I know. Odd, really. They were part of her trousseau. It was all up there in the attic, packed for her honeymoon. They were going to be married three days later. I found the whole story online in the transcribed memoir of the old biddy who lived next door." Vicki turned to Sinclair. "You should read it. She has a lot to say about your ancestors. Temperance married five times and his wives kept disappearing."

Katherine shuddered slightly. "The curse. Or whatever it is. The Drummonds can never find happiness. But we're going to change all that, so Sinclair can find happiness." She beamed a smile at him.

Sinclair grimaced, now resting his elbows above his head on either side of the door frame, which provided an eye-popping view of his powerful muscles against the sleeves of his shirt. Annie dragged her tormented gaze in the other direction.

"I'll make sure he finds happiness at the dance, at least." Vicki fingered another dress, a frothy pink taffeta with seed pearls encrusting the bodice. "I won't try these on now, though. Another time. I'm pretty sure at least one will fit fine with no alteration."

"Let's go have coffee," said Sinclair gruffly.

Annie was glad to get away from the spectacle of Vicki handling the dresses. She shouldn't think of them as *her* dresses, because they weren't, but she'd felt proprietary about them ever since she'd tried that one on and been so entranced by it. It was even less encouraging to learn they'd belonged to some long-ago woman whose life had gone off the rails. How likely was a woman to find happiness by running away in a stolen carriage?

She'd never find out. She wasn't nearly daring enough for that kind of high-risk endeavor. That's why she'd be watching other people's exploits over the rim of her teacup rather than living on the edge.

"You're going to that party, Annie." Vicki's whisper sliced into her ear as the taller woman slid past her in the hallway.

"What?" Annie froze. But Vicki had already disappeared into the living room with Katherine and was talking about something else.

Six

"But I can't." Annie faced Katherine and Vicki over the pile of fresh peas she'd been shelling for Katherine's dinner. It was 5:00 p.m. and Vicki should have been getting dressed for the dance.

"Let me guess, you have nothing to wear." Vicki crossed her arms over her chest.

"Not just that. I'm not invited, and I don't..." She hesitated, not really wanting to say it out loud.

"Don't belong there?" asked Katherine, with perfect accuracy. "Nonsense. It's a party, and it's huge. Over five hundred people. Sinclair can't go alone because it's a couples theme and they have all these silly activities planned."

Annie's eyes widened. Romantic activities? Was Sinclair's mom actually trying to set her up with him?

"Of course you and Sinclair won't do anything romantic." She laughed at such an outlandish idea. Well, that answered one question. "But I'm sure you'll have a good time. I know he'll refuse to go if he isn't required to escort anyone, and why shouldn't Cinderella go to the ball for a change?" She laughed again, obviously delighted with the idea Vicki had planted in her mind. She turned to Vicki. "Do you need more aspirin, dear?"

"Probably. Maybe I should just take the whole bottle." Vicki had been complaining of a headache since mid-afternoon. "Then again, when I get these headaches no medicine even helps. I'm out of business for the rest of the day."

"Poor thing. Why don't you go lie down?"

"Oh, no," Vicki said quickly, then held her head. "Helping make Annie gorgeous will take my mind off the pain." She flashed a smile at Annie that made an entirely different kind of pain shoot through her. Why was Vicki trying so hard to humiliate her?

"I really don't think it's a good idea." Annie wished she could put her foot down. Surely attending a big, fancy party couldn't possibly be described as part of a housekeeper's duties. "I'm sure Sinclair would rather go alone."

She knew that part was true. He wanted to pretend he'd never kissed her. Never made crazy, unexpected love to her and breathed hot moans in her ear. Bitter disappointment trickled through her—again.

"Nonsense. And you'll enjoy it, Annie. It'll be the party of the summer. They're probably spending two million on it. Think of it as an experience, rather like an adventure vacation. Now, we need to find you a dress. I think I have a loose-fitting Zang Toi that's a bit big for me…"

"We won't need that." Vicki put a proprietary arm

around Annie, who shrank from her. "She can wear one of the dresses from the abandoned trousseau."

Katherine looked doubtfully at Annie's waist, which she instinctively sucked in. "I'm not sure those will fit."

"I suspect Annie's a lot trimmer than her usual attire would have us believe. Let's go have a look." Vicki marched purposefully down the corridor, with Katherine in hot pursuit, leaving Annie no choice but to slouch after them.

She couldn't even begin to imagine the look she'd see on Sinclair's face when they paraded her in front of him wearing one of the dresses that had already caused so much trouble. He'd be appalled. He'd probably think it was her idea. Some crude scheme to ensnare him.

Maybe he'd point-blank refuse to go.

"I think the silvery gray one will look lovely against her complexion."

Did silvery gray look good against beetroot? Annie avoided looking in the large mirror on the front of the wardrobe. Vicki held up the long dress with its low-cut princess neckline and huge skirt.

"Of course, they would have worn it with a crinoline and loads of extra petticoats, but we'll spare you that. Especially since we don't have any. We'll wait outside while you put it on."

Annie was grateful for the slight nod to her modesty. She climbed out of her familiar shirt and khakis with a sinking feeling. If this didn't fit, they'd only make her try on another. Worst-case scenario, she'd end up in the peacock dress she'd worn already, with them wondering why it looked so crumpled.

The dress was quite heavy, with built-in boning at the waist and yards of expensive silk. The short, puffy sleeves hugged her arms quite tightly, but there was no way she could do up the long line of buttons down the back by herself. "Um…"

"Need help?" Vicki was right outside the door. She opened it without an invitation. "Oh, yes."

Annie felt hot and flustered under their rather stunned gazes. "I must look very silly."

"Nonsense. You look lovely." Katherine frowned. "What are we going to do with her hair?" Her eyes raked over Annie like she was a mannequin.

"Got to be an updo." Vicki squinted at her. "I have some pins and hairspray in my room. And some earrings."

They buttoned her into the dress, which fit almost perfectly. The original owner must have been quite chunky by Victorian standards, if this fit her corseted waist. The bodice hugged Annie's cleavage in an embarrassing but flattering way, especially after Katherine convinced her to abandon her bra. Vicki fussed over her hair, creating tiny finger coils that framed her temples, and Katherine lent her a pair of pewter ballet flats.

"Won't I be overdressed?" The silk skirt fell to the floor.

"A lady can never be overdressed." Katherine eyed her with approval. "Especially not when she looks fabulous. Goodness, I'd never have guessed you had such a lovely figure. You should show it off more."

Great. Now they'd probably get her a French maid's uniform to wear while performing her duties.

"Maybe we'd better make sure Sinclair looks presentable." Vicki glanced toward the door.

"Oh, don't worry about him. He always looks good.

Horribly unfair. I don't know how he stays so tanned, either. He always seems to have his face in his laptop."

"I suspect Sinclair of having a secret life." Vicki snuck a wink at Annie, who pretended not to notice.

"Where he's out lying in the sun?"

"Or running along the beach with the wind in his hair." Vicki laughed. "I have a feeling most people only see a tiny part of the real Sinclair."

"Hmm." Katherine looked doubtful. "Well, as long as the other parts are going to give me a grandchild before I get too old and decrepit, that's fine. He doesn't know he's going with Annie instead yet, does he?"

"I haven't breathed a word. I think we should stay out of the way until the last minute, then surprise him with her." Annie cringed, but had long given up trying to shape the evening's events. All she could do now was brace herself.

Three hours later, the sound of Sinclair's tread on the stairs made her gut clench into a fist. He'd been in his room almost since lunch, supposedly working. He hadn't heard about Vicki's supposed headache. Or that he was about to see his housekeeper dressed like some sacrificial virgin—except without the virgin part.

"Come, stand here. I can't wait to see his face." Vicki prodded her into position in the alcove between the living room and the front hallway. Annie wished she could warn him somehow. What look would they all see on his face? Horror, quite likely. Then maybe disgust.

"Sinclair, darling, do come into the living room for a cocktail before you go." His mom winked at Annie.

"Is Vicki ready?" His world-weary tone carried

through the house along with the sound of his footfalls on the old oak boards.

"Not exactly." Vicki crossed her arms and looked smug. She held a finger over her lips. Annie wished she could dive behind the sofa. Her heart rate increased as Sinclair's movements grew closer. By the time he reached the door, her heart was pounding so hard she worried the whalebone stays in her bodice might burst and release her braless breasts just in time for his entrance.

"Come in, Sinclair." She heard his mom from outside the room.

"Why's everyone acting so strange?" His deep voice sent a ripple of anticipation—richly mingled with dread—right through her.

He rounded the corner and looked up, at her. Frozen to the spot and unable to think at all, let alone utter a word, she watched his reaction. Astonishment, sure. Disbelief. Her face heated as he took in her hair, her earrings, the subtle makeup Vicki had painstakingly applied. Then his gaze dropped lower, almost imperceptibly grazing her cleavage and the nipped-in waistline of the dress. Her breasts swelled against the snug neckline, responding to the desire that flashed in his eyes. Or was that alarm?

"Annie, you look stunning." His compliment sounded cool and composed, as if he'd expected to see her standing there dressed for the party.

"Vicki isn't well," she rushed to explain. "And they didn't think you'd go if you were alone, so they insisted that I..." She wanted to let him know this wasn't her idea.

"Vicki's loss is my gain."

His expression was unreadable. She reminded herself it was simply a polite response, something he might say to a friend of his mother's. No doubt he didn't want to betray his horror to the others or they'd suspect there was some reason he felt uncomfortable going with her. Beyond the obvious reason that she was supposed to be waxing the furniture, not waltzing with the boss.

"It seemed such a shame to waste the invitation." Katherine picked a speck of imaginary lint from his spotless tux. "And why shouldn't Annie get to have some fun for a change? You will make sure she has a good time, won't you?"

"Of course." He didn't take his eyes off Annie. "It would be my pleasure."

There was an oddly flat tone to his voice.

I'm sorry. She tried to say it with her eyes. He must be appalled at the prospect of spending the evening with her. Maybe he thought she'd try to rekindle the flame of lust that had singed them both so badly.

"Why don't we all have a gin and tonic?" Vicki moved toward the drinks cabinet.

"No, thanks." Sinclair and Annie said it in unison. A moment of awkward silence turned into a nervous laugh. "We should get going," said Sinclair. He probably wanted to get out of there and get this whole charade over with as quickly as possible.

Annie gathered her impressive skirts. Hopefully she wouldn't trip over them and fall flat on her face. She headed for the side door, through the kitchen, but Katherine pulled open the formal front door they rarely used. "This way tonight. You look far too elegant to sneak out the side door." She now had to negotiate the rather uneven brick steps, and an equally hazardous slate walkway, and was almost breaking a sweat by the time they reached the driveway. Sinclair's black BMW gleamed golden in the low rays of sunlight sneaking through the tall hedges. She walked toward it until she realized there was a silver Bentley sitting a little farther up the drive.

"We're being driven to the event." He spoke coolly. "Mom is always very cautious about drinking and driving."

A uniformed driver emerged and held open one of the rear doors. Annie's spirits sank when she realized they wouldn't be alone even long enough for her to plead innocence in this whole caper. She managed to climb in, pulling her long skirt behind her and arranging it around her legs.

Sinclair entered on the other side and sat next to her. The rear seat was spacious enough to leave room for another person between them, but the space quickly filled with tension.

The driver climbed into his seat and started the engine, then started to speak with a heavy Brooklyn accent. "I'll be waiting there for you tonight, so you can leave any time you want. Sounds like quite the party, from the talk at the depot. Everyone wants a limo tonight. We could have rented this one three times over." Annie pictured people scrambling to rent fabulous limousines before the town ran dry of them. Who knew such problems existed?

Sinclair glanced sideways at her. Probably wondering why she was there instead of Vicki.

"Vicki complained of a headache since lunch." She felt the need to explain in a way that wouldn't reveal the whole situation to the rather chatty driver. "She seemed really keen for me to come."

"She's never had so much as a hangnail in all the years I've known her." He met her gaze. Her breath hitched at the warmth in his dark eyes. "I suspect she has an ulterior motive."

"I was wondering about that." She fingered the beading at her waistline. "It was all her idea."

"Doesn't surprise me in the least."

Annie hesitated. It was hard to be secretive and frank at the same time. But she did wonder if Sinclair had laughingly told Vicki about their...misadventure. "I didn't say anything to her at all, about, you know."

He frowned for a moment. "Of course you didn't." She waited for him to say that he'd also kept quiet. "She probably has her own agenda. Maybe she's trying to avoid someone who'll be there."

Annie nodded. "Could be." She couldn't figure Vicki out at all, but if she'd teased her about liking Sinclair, she wouldn't be surprised if she'd done the same to him.

Apparently he wasn't going to reveal anything either way.

He looked breathtakingly handsome in his tux. The crisp, white shirt collar emphasized the hard, bronzed lines of his chin and cheekbones. She'd have loved to drink in the vision of him but had to make do with surreptitious glances.

She risked another sneak peak, enjoying the set of his broad shoulders against the luxurious leather seat of the car. "Your mom looks better every day."

"Yes, thank God. She really does seem to be on the mend. The doctors said it will be months before she's fully recovered, though. Her liver and kidneys shut down and her immune system almost gave up. She's very lucky to be here. This whole thing with the cup is keeping her at home, too, which is good. Normally she's traveling all over the world, which the doctors told her not to do until her immune system is up to speed. I'm sure that's the only reason she's not in Scotland storming the baronial halls of that particular Drummond."

Annie laughed. "I can't believe how much stuff is in that one attic. It could take a lifetime to go through it." She glanced at the driver. Maybe it wasn't wise to reveal their treasure trove to a total stranger.

"That's good. It will keep Mom safely in Dog Harbor longer." His wry smile sent a flash of warmth to her heart. He settled his broad hand on the soft seat and for a second she imagined it resting on her thigh, only inches away, hidden beneath the dress's layer of silk.

"It's downright strange how well that dress fits you. Almost like it was made for you."

"Weird, huh? The original owner would have worn all kinds of undergarments to get it this shape. I just have a narrow waist." She shrugged. "It seems wrong to wear something that's really an antique. It must ruin the fabric. But Vicki kept saying that clothes are for wearing, not storing in boxes. And she is an antiques dealer so I suppose she knows what she's talking about." At least she wasn't trying to steal them and sell them on eBay.

"I agree. And maybe it was made for you, if the unseen powers of the universe that my mother's grown so fond of are really at work." His dark gaze sent a shiver of strange emotion though her. Did those same mysterious forces throw them into each others' arms? Maybe they were meant to be together and Vicki was a cleverly disguised fairy godmother who'd conjured her into this finery so she could go to the ball with her prince.

Which meant this Bentley might turn into a pump-kin at midnight.

"What are you laughing at?"

"I don't know. Trying to dissolve the tension." She snuck a glance at the driver, wondering if he was a rat transformed into a man by the wave of a magic wand. She didn't want him to know she wasn't supposed to be here. For all he knew, she was some heiress, out on a date with wealthy bachelor Sinclair Drummond.

How was he going to introduce her to people? *This is Annie Sullivan, my housekeeper* probably wouldn't go over too well. *This is my old friend Annie? Let me introduce you to the love of my life?* Another stray gig-gle bubbled in her chest.

Being so close to him made her giddy. Her skirt poufed out until it was resting on the leg of his black pants, caressing his thigh. Her fingers longed to do the same. He looked so relaxed and at ease. Maybe he was happy to be here with her? Maybe he'd secretly orches-trated the whole thing, with Vicki as his accomplice, so he could take her to the ball as his date without alarm-ing his still-weak mom?

One look at his somber face in profile, staring out the window, purged that thought from her mind. He'd probably rather be anywhere than here, with her. He hadn't even responded to her comment about dissolv-ing tension, perhaps preferring a sturdy barrier of angst between them to easy intimacy. She had to stay focused on getting through this evening with a minimum of hu-miliation and hurt, and that meant keeping her emotions firmly under wraps.

They arrived at the beachfront mansion in less than ten minutes, and the Bentley pulled into the circular driveway in a line of cars depositing their occupants in front of a large stone house. Artfully placed lighting lit up the night and sparkled off the elegant gowns and pearly smiles of the glamorous people around them. The driver helped Annie out of the car and she thanked him.

Sinclair rounded the car and took her arm in his. The increased closeness made her feel panicky. What if she couldn't resist the urge to throw her arms around his neck and kiss him? Experience had already proven she could go completely mad in his presence.

"Don't be nervous. They're all just human under the crazy outfits." Sinclair's rough whisper in her ear startled her, then made her chuckle. How sweet of him to try to relax her.

"I may well have the craziest outfit here." Her big, pale dress stood out amongst a lot of sleek dark gowns.

Sinclair stopped and looked at her for a moment as if contemplating whether this was true. More cars pulled in and guests swirled around them. "You're the most stunning woman here, and you look unbelievably beautiful in that dress."

The murmur of conversations and the purr of expensive engines faded into silence as his words took over her brain. Had he really said that, or had she imagined it? His dark eyes rested on hers for a second longer, stealing the last of her breath. For a second she thought she might fall down unconscious.

"Sinclair, darling!" Reality sucked her back into its jaws as a very tall blonde woman threw her arms around Sinclair. They bumped into Annie, almost knocking her to the ground. "And my husband was worried you wouldn't come. I knew you'd grace us with your austere and magnificent presence." She kissed him on both cheeks. Annie simply stared.

"And who is this damsel on your arm this evening?" The blonde peered at Annie with large, blue eyes.

"I'm pleased to be escorting the lovely Annie Sullivan."

"A pleasure to make your acquaintance, Miss Sullivan." The hostess shook her hand firmly. "You look familiar. Have we met before?"

Annie hesitated. She'd likely served this woman finger sandwiches or taken her coat for hanging. But she couldn't tell. These very rich, emaciated blonde women all looked alike after a while. "Perhaps."

"Do head around to the tent and enjoy some drinks. Henry's madcap festivities will be starting soon but we need everyone a little tipsy first."

"Happy anniversary, Jessica." Sinclair smiled. Then he took Annie's arm again and led her along a path lit with glowing lanterns toward the rear of the house. Strains of music floated on the air, mingling with the tinkle of polite laughter. "She's an old friend of my mom's," Sinclair murmured, once they were out of earshot.

"Thanks for not introducing me as your housekeeper. Though I don't know why that would be embarrassing, since it is my job after all."

"You're not here as my housekeeper. You're here as my date." He gave her a stern look. She wasn't sure whether to take it seriously. Was this a date with the Annie who'd writhed on the spare bed with him, or the one who was under orders to pretend it had never happened? His arm linked with hers felt proprietary, like he was taking charge of the situation, which was fine with her. She never felt Sinclair would try to take advantage of her.

What a shame.

A waiter swept toward them with a tray of champagne glasses. Sinclair took one and handed it to her. The glass was cold against her hand, in sharp contrast to her hot skin. People swirled around them on the large terrace. Hanging lanterns illuminated the night enough for them to make each other out, but the garden beyond was cloaked in velvety darkness. The unknown. A band, tucked away somewhere, launched into a swingy jazz number that made the very air throb with anticipation.

She took the tiniest sip of her champagne, and the bubbles tickled her tongue. Sinclair took a manlier drink from his glass. Muted light played across his hard features. His eyes glittered, dark and unreadable, as they rested on her face.

"I've never seen a woman look more radiant, Annie." He spoke plainly, with no hint of joking or exaggeration.

Her bodice suddenly felt tight as her chest swelled. "I don't think I've seen a man look more handsome." She tried to laugh off his comment with an offhand one of her own.

But Sinclair didn't even seem to notice what she said. He frowned. "Why do you hide your beauty?"

"I don't hide anything. You see me every day, or at least when you're out at the house. I'm hardly wearing a mask. That's the real me. This is the one that Vicki decorated for the party."

He took a sip of his champagne. "You're right, of course. And in fact, I think you're even more beautiful when you're not dressed up like a visiting princess." His words sank in and her breath stuck in her throat.

"It's refreshing to see someone who isn't afraid to be her natural self and not try to enhance something that's already lovely."

She blinked. "I'm sure the folks at L.L. Bean will be glad to hear that." She managed a smile. "I bet they'd hate to hear I was abandoning my familiar khakis and Oxford shirts for vintage prom dresses."

"Then I'm with them. I like the authentic Annie."

"Your mom didn't think I'd fit in these dresses. I think the general consensus is that my usual look makes me appear shapeless."

"I heartily disagree, but on the other hand it does leave something to the imagination." A tiny smile crossed his mouth. "And some surprises to discover."

Was he flirting with her? It certainly felt like flirting, not that she had much experience to rely on.

"I think you've discovered most of my surprises." There, she'd said it. She'd been burning to bring up that afternoon. There was no way she could get through this night pretending it had never happened.

"I doubt that very much." His gaze lingered on hers for a moment, heating her blood. "In fact I feel confident that I only scratched the surface."

The silence thickened with the suggestion that he'd like to return for another journey of discovery. Annie sucked in a breath, which wasn't easy in her tight bodice. She'd certainly be up for a voyage into the dark and mysterious lands of Sinclair, but only if it wasn't another accident. She wasn't sure she could handle trying to pretend something like that never happened again.

On the other hand, if it was mutually desired, and mutually agreed upon...

She sipped her champagne and the bubbles tickled

the tip of her tongue again. "What kind of activities do they have planned for tonight?"

"Are you nervous?" Humor shone in his eyes.

"A little. Especially since they want us half-cocked before we start. That sounds rather dangerous."

"I promise I'll protect you." He raised his glass and sipped, looking at her steadily over the rim.

A sense of clear and present danger swelled in the air. "It's entirely possible that you're exactly what I need protecting from. After all, we didn't need too much encouragement that one time."

His gaze darkened slightly. "True. Tonight I'll be a gentleman if it kills me."

"Shame." She said it boldly, not wanting him to think she wasn't interested. She'd already gone out on a limb, so why not keep going until it snapped? Maybe the champagne was making her reckless.

A smile played around his eyes, crinkling the skin in that way she found so adorable. "If you don't want me to be a gentleman, I'm sure that can also be arranged."

"Good. I think I'd prefer a dashing rake." Now she was flirting.

"Is that so? In that case, let's top off your champagne so I can more easily take advantage of you." He gestured to a passing waiter, who readily obliged. How had she drunk more than half a glass already?

"Sinclair, how did you sneak past me? I've been lying in wait for you all night." A tall brunette materialized out of the night air and breathed in his ear. "Your mother told me you're in town for the summer. I do hope you'll have time to come out on my new yacht."

"Dara, this is Annie, Annie, Dara." Annie thrust out a hand so that at least one of them couldn't be accused of rudeness. Dara had barely glanced at her. Now she reluctantly gave her a limp handshake. At least Annie didn't recognize her from any social events at the house. "I'm going to be very busy this summer. Annie has me all tied up." He spoke with a straight face, but a hint of suggestion in his voice.

Dara's mouth opened like a fish. "Really." She took a longer look at Annie. "Well, if you change your mind." She flounced off, looking distinctly irritated.

"That was fun." Sinclair sipped his champagne and surveyed her with narrowed eyes.

"You're naughty."

"And enjoying it. Let's dance."

It wasn't a question. His sudden, sturdy grip around her waist swept her toward a wooden dance floor set up under an elegant canopy on the lawn. They moved through a crowd of laughing, chatting people, and handed their glasses to one of the many waiters before climbing onto the dance floor just as a song was ending. The band was a big jazz ensemble with a stunning singer. "Oh, my God, is that Natalie Cole?"

"Probably."

Laughing, Annie let him pull her into his arms as the singer started into a sultry number about a broken heart. He wound one hand firmly around her and took her hand with the other, and pulled her into a dance. Her feet followed his effortlessly, as if she already knew the steps. The thundering drumbeat and mellow pulse of the saxophone flowed through her, drawing her around the dance floor as if she did this every day. She could feel the smile glowing on her face as Sinclair twirled her through the crowds, her long dress flying out around her. His gaze stayed fixed on hers the whole time, capturing her attention and daring her to look away.

Her breaths came faster and faster as the pace of the song picked up and they swept across the floor with bold dance steps. Sinclair's muscular hands guided her, making her feel pliable and athletic, almost fluid, moving in time to the music.

The singer launched into an impassioned plea to her lover, begging him to come back and make her whole. Annie let herself ride on the wave of emotion her voice created among the dancers. Her heart seemed to pound in time with the bold blasts from the trumpet as the song rose to a crescendo and Sinclair held her tighter against his chest.

Their faces grew closer, gazes still locked in a mute challenge. He was taller than her, but if he leaned down he could kiss her right on the lips.

Her mouth started to quiver in anticipation. Surely he couldn't tantalize her like this and not kiss her? Her entire body felt alive with desire for him, her nipples pressing relentlessly against the tight bodice of her dress. The song ended with a sudden flourish and she waited in an agony of excitement for his lips to touch hers.

Seven

But they didn't.

He pulled back from her, shoved a hand through his hair and glanced across the dance floor. Annie stood there stunned. The flowing motion had ceased so abruptly that she felt like a fish suddenly thrown up on dry sand, wondering what happened. Blinking, she stepped back, trying to regain her composure. She bumped into someone and had to turn and apologize. When she turned back, Sinclair was staring into the distance with a face like honed granite.

"What is it?" She had to say something, if only to reassure herself that she still had the power of speech.

"Nothing." He frowned. "Let's go get some air."

It was hard to imagine that they weren't getting air already, since they were outdoors. As they walked across the lawn, fresh glasses of champagne in their hands, Annie realized that the "lake" was actually Long

Island Sound, stretching out before them in a gleaming sheet, with the full moon glowing on its surface like an oversized silver Christmas ornament.

"Do you think they booked this moon along with the band?"

"Quite likely." He looked out over the water. "Whatever they paid, it was worth the money." He sipped his champagne, silent for a moment. He looked anything but relaxed. The buildup to their non-kiss had tightened all her muscles and sent blood flowing to places she wasn't usually aware of. She was on edge and fired up with anticipation that had no place to go, and he looked the same.

Should she tell him she didn't regret their wild afternoon in bed? Right now she didn't. It had awakened her to a new sensual side of herself.

"What is your ambition in life, Annie?" He turned to her suddenly, fixing her with the full force of his dark gaze.

Was this some kind of test? If she answered wrong would his estimation of her plummet even lower? "To own my own home." She answered with the simple truth. It was a small dream, and an old-fashioned one, but it had guided her decisions ever since she'd left home at age twenty-one.

"Why don't you buy one?" He frowned slightly.

She laughed. "They cost money."

"You earn a good salary."

"Yes, living in *your* home and taking care of it. If I moved I'd be out of a job."

"So your job in my house is preventing you from fulfilling your dream?"

"Not at all. I'm saving the money so that when I'm

ready I can buy it. I'm not nearly there yet, in case you're worried about your floors going unpolished." She meant it as a joke, but it came out almost scolding. "It's just something I've always wanted. I grew up in a big house filled with people. My grandmother's house." Her Connecticut was very different from the one Sinclair had lived in with his ex-wife Muffy. There were no shady lawns or million-dollar mansions on her street, in one of the grimmer parts of the old industrial city. "My parents and sister still live there. It's like a trap or something. My sister moved away when she got married and had a child, but now she's divorced and back there again. My dad's been on disability for decades and just watches TV all day. He could work if he wanted to, but he'd rather just sit around. My mom, on the other hand, works all day and night just to get out of the house." She raised a brow. "That's probably what I'd be doing, too, if I was still there. I want to have my own space where I can do what I like."

"And that's your only goal?" Apparently that wasn't enough for Sinclair Drummond. Which was hardly surprising, given all he'd already achieved in his own life.

"I'm thinking more about my career. I'm planning to take evening classes and learn about running a business. I'd like to be self-employed eventually. Maybe even own a shop. Being a housekeeper isn't a highly transferrable career in this day and age." She smiled.

"I suppose it's not easy to find someone with more houses than they have need of." He looked as if he was going to smile, but he didn't. If anything he looked pained. Perhaps he'd been hoping she'd prove herself worthy of him with a grand ambition. He must be cruelly disappointed by her simple aspirations.

"What's your dream?" She'd never have dared to ask him if they weren't here tonight, in the silver-edged darkness.

Sinclair hesitated for a moment. Frowned. "I don't know anymore. I used to want a family life, children, all that, but now I know that's not for me."

"How do you know that? You've never tried." Her indignation made her sound abrupt.

"To have a family you have to be married, and my two efforts in that direction have demonstrated that I'm not a suitable husband."

"Maybe they weren't suitable wives." She cocked her chin.

"Not for me, apparently." He looked out over Long Island Sound. "I won't make that same mistake again."

"That seems a real shame. You're far too young to swear off relationships. Besides, you can easily afford a few more divorces." Her joke was meant to defuse the tension, but the haunted look he gave her only ratcheted it higher. "Not that you'd ever have another, of course."

"I guarantee that I won't. Since I have no intention of getting married again." He drained his champagne glass and stared out over the dark water. "You should marry."

"What? Why?" His odd statement shocked her. The idea that he even had any thoughts on the subject made her uneasy.

"You're nurturing and thoughtful. You'd be a good mother. Someone would be very lucky to have you as a partner." He glanced at her, then looked away again, as if something on the black-velvet horizon held his attention.

"You make me sound rather dull. Not the kind of

person who goes to elegant dances wearing a vintage dress." She teased him. He was right, of course.

"Not at all, because quite obviously you are the kind of person who lights up the night at an occasion like this." His gaze swept quietly over her, stirring a flurry of arousal. His eyes lingered on her lips, which twitched involuntarily, still hungry for the kiss they never got.

She really needed to distract herself from wanting to kiss him. Although her body thought it was a good idea, her mind knew better. It would only make her life more complicated. After all, he'd made it clear he didn't want a relationship with her—or anyone—so where could it lead?

Still, why did he have to have such a sensual mouth? His lips were quite full, with a graceful arch on the top, in tantalizing contrast to the masculine jut of his cheekbones and jaw, and the aristocratic profile of his nose. Frankly, his lips begged to be kissed.

And having kissed him once, she knew just how soft and yet how firm they'd be as she pressed her lips against them.

"So, why don't you want to marry again?" That line of questioning should kill any hint of romance.

He raised a brow. "Isn't it obvious?"

"Because your marriages failed? I'd imagine that would be off-putting, but it didn't stop Elizabeth Taylor." She smiled. "I bet if you found the right person you'd get it right this time."

I could be that right person.

Her brain spat out the thought entirely against her will. She spat it right back. She was trying to crush her romantic aspirations toward Sinclair, not stoke them.

"Maybe you need to figure out exactly what went

wrong. Did you ever do that?" She was pretty darn curious, for sure.

"It's easy. We wanted different things. My first wife, Muffy..." He hesitated.

Of course she was called Muffy. She probably wore pink twinsets with little whales embroidered on them.

"We were together all through college and did everything together. We got married the summer after graduation, and both of our families were thrilled. We bought a lovely house in Connecticut and I thought we'd live happily ever after. Then she decided she wanted to pursue a doctorate in modern languages at Yale, then she wanted to become a professor, then she wanted to take a position at a university in Peru, and by that point we'd realized we were two different people on entirely different courses and we went our separate ways. She teaches at a university in Argentina. It seemed like she changed into a completely different person after I married her."

"You never considered moving away with her?"

"No. I have my life here, my business. I don't want to spend my time traveling around the world." He looked out over the Sound. "I decided right then that I'd never get serious about someone who's just starting out in life and has no idea what they want yet. One of the things I liked about Diana was that she had her own established PR business and had built a full life for herself. I was pretty confident she wasn't going to throw it all away and move to Tibet to join a monastery." He smiled wryly. "And that was where our problems started."

"She joined a monastery?" Annie's eyes widened.

"No. Her life was so full that there was no room for me and my life in it. I didn't want to fly around the country each weekend going to weddings and parties and visiting friends and clients. If I didn't do those things, I didn't see my wife. Still, I was determined to make it work so I let her do her thing while I did mine." He frowned. "I started to believe that was how successful marriages worked. I didn't have a very good example to follow. My parents led almost entirely separate lives during my childhood. That's one of the reasons we have several houses." He sighed. "But Diana found someone else."

"Oh." She knew that already. Her infidelity had been the grounds for the divorce. "I'm sorry."

"So, you see, I'm too inflexible. I wasn't willing to live their lives and they weren't willing to live mine. Maybe I should just get a dog?" He raised an eyebrow, and humor sparkled in his eyes.

"I don't know. That's a big commitment. All that walking. And what if you want to go to the beach and he wants to go to the park?" She giggled. There was something strangely intimate in Sinclair trusting her with the story of his failed relationships. She felt closer to him than ever before.

"You're right. And I travel a lot."

"You'd have to get your housekeeper to walk it." She tilted her head. "Housekeepers can handle that kind of responsibility."

"Sounds like I need a housekeeper more than I need a wife."

"Lucky thing you already have one." She sipped her champagne. "And apparently she's a housekeeper with benefits." She raised a brow.

Sinclair's shocked expression made her regret her little jibe. Then his face softened and the look he gave her made her stomach do a somersault. "Which proves, I suppose, that just having a housekeeper isn't enough." His voice was gruff, rich with all the emotion he kept buried beneath his chiseled and polished surface.

"You're a unique individual." She tried to look arch, like the heroine in a regency novel. Though she wasn't really sure what arch looked like so she probably didn't pull it off. "You need a very special housekeeper." Clearly she was tipsy. Or the dress had once again unleashed a part of her that dared to do things the usual Annie wouldn't dream of.

"What are you two doing all the way over here?" A voice beckoned to them across the lawn. "Come back to civilization for some oysters."

"Oysters." Sinclair laughed. "Just what we need."

"Aren't they supposed to be an aphrodisiac?"

"Exactly. Do you and I really need an aphrodisiac?" His gaze lingered on her face long enough to heat her skin.

No. We don't need one. Desire flashed between them like electric current, and he'd just admitted he could feel it. "I've never tried oysters."

"Never? Then let's go fix that terrible omission." He held his arm out for her to take it. A gesture that was formal but breathtakingly intimate at the same time. When she slid her arm through his, she could swear she felt the heat of him through his elegant suit, though maybe she imagined it. She was so overstimulated by his presence that she couldn't trust her senses anymore. She knew that a muscled body, capable of passion and abandon no one here would have expected, lay beneath his formal attire. Did anyone here imagine what had gone on between them?

Couples strolled on the lawn and the terrace, arm in arm like them, laughing. Everyone seemed to be paired up, but that was the theme of the party. Caterers in black-and-white uniforms moved among them, brandishing silver platters piled high with oyster shells. Tables for two had sprung up all over the lawn like mushrooms after a rain, each set with two delicate patterned plates and oyster forks. A bucket of fresh champagne stood beside each table, and chairs decorated with ribbons beckoned each couple to sit. Sinclair pulled out a chair for her and she arranged her wide skirt around her legs.

Three sauce bowls, each with a tiny spoon, sat in the middle of the table, next to a dish of lemon wedges. Sinclair poured them each a flute of champagne. The opened oysters glowed intriguingly in the moonlight in their mother-of-pearl-lined shells. He picked up a shell and spooned one of the sauces onto it. "Open your mouth."

She obeyed, her stomach clenching slightly, either because of the strange food or the prospect of Sinclair feeding it to her—or both. He tipped the shell toward her mouth and she gently sucked. The cool, oceany taste of the oyster met with a pleasantly sharp explosion of picante sauce on her tongue.

"Swallow."

She swallowed, blinking at the strange sensation of the smooth oyster sliding down her throat. "That was different."

Sinclair smiled. "Now you feed me one."

"My duties as a housekeeper keep expanding in strange directions." She glanced flirtatiously at him. She wasn't sure why she kept reminding him—and her-

self—that he was her employer, but somehow it seemed
preferable to having them both forget again. It made
whatever romance they did share feel more...real.

"You're not here as my housekeeper." Sinclair obviously didn't find comfort in her words. "But feed me
an oyster anyway." His voice contained a hint of suggestion that made her skin tingle with awareness. She
reached for the plate and took one of the pearly shells.
She surveyed the sauces. One looked tomatoey, like
a cocktail sauce. One was thinner and a little darker,
probably hot sauce. The other had herbs floating in it—
garlic? She decided to go classic and squeezed a spritz
of lemon onto the fish, then held it out. Sinclair's lips
struggled with a slight smile as he opened them for her
to tip the contents of the shell into his mouth. Her fingers trembled but she managed to hold it steady as he
slurped the oyster gracefully into his mouth and swallowed it. "Delicious."

The satisfied look on his face suggested that it wasn't
only their appetizer that he spoke about. Some strange
place way below her belly button shimmied in response.
Was this the aphrodisiac effect of the oysters?

"Your turn." Their champagne sat untouched as he
fed her another oyster, then she fed him. Then he caught
hold of her fingers that proffered the shell and kissed
them, sending sparks of arousal dancing up her arm.

"You're glowing tonight." He spoke softly, serious.

"Like the oyster shells." She said the first thing that
came to mind. His compliment shocked and embarrassed her.

Those adorable smile crinkles showed around his
eyes. "In most of the women I know, modesty sounds
like they're fishing for compliments. In you it's far more

annoying because I suspect you really mean it." He kissed her fingertips again before letting them go.

"No one growing up in my family could suffer from a swelled head for long."

He leaned forward. "I don't know anything about your family, except that you need to buy your own house so you don't have to live with them anymore."

She laughed. "They're not that bad. Just loud and bossy and funny. They're nice, really, except Granny when she's in one of her moods. She's the dictator of the family and what she says, goes."

"Partly because she owns the house everyone lives in."

"Exactly." She smiled. "You have personal experience with how that works."

"I don't have moods," he protested. His eyes glittered with amusement.

"Not often, anyway," she teased. "But if you did I'd have to put up with them, wouldn't I?"

"Definitely not. I don't encourage people to slink about like mute sheep. I wouldn't have much of a business if everyone yessed me to death."

"I suppose you're right." She had tiptoed around him for a long time. Maybe that's why he hadn't seemed to notice her before. Judging from his past wives, he was attracted to rather strong-minded women—even if he couldn't actually stay married to them. "I'll make a point of being more assertive. Then again, I'm not sure I need to be, since I do everything my way and you all seem to be happy anyway."

A smile crept across his mouth. "Sounds like the ideal state of affairs. Obviously your way is perfect."

He tilted his head slightly, and held her gaze with those relentless dark eyes. "For me, anyway."

Annie's chest tightened inside her elegant gown. This sounded like some kind of major declaration. Or was it simply dinner-party chatter? She didn't have enough experience to tell the difference. And Sinclair's eyes were having a very unsettling effect on her.

He lifted both of their glasses and handed one to her. "To perfection. Long may it reign in castle Drummond." She smiled and clinked her glass against his. The champagne contrasted pleasurably with the smooth saltiness of the oyster.

"Castle Drummond. I like that. The house doesn't have a name, does it?"

"We've always called it Dog Harbor, after the town. It should, though. Anything that's hung in there for three hundred years should have a name."

"Especially if it's built of wood. I can't believe those ceiling beams in the attic. That house was built to stand the test of time. Do you think part of that old cup is really up there somewhere?"

He shrugged. "Could well be. It has no value or function that would encourage anyone to sell it over the years, so unless it was thrown away at some point, it's probably in there somewhere."

He fed her another oyster, and she shivered slightly as the cool, liquidy flesh slid down her throat. The tender look in his eyes made the gesture seem almost protective. *Don't get carried away! This is just one night.*

It was hard not to, though. She picked up another oyster and fed it to him. He held her gaze as he pulled it into his mouth, and a corresponding flash of awareness lit up her secret places. Energy was gathering here, swirling around them, drawing them closer together.

A waiter arrived at the table with an empty wine bottle and a broad smile. Annie and Sinclair both looked at him curiously. Then he pulled out two leaves of delicate paper and two golden pencils. "You are hereby invited to write a message to each other. Preferably something you'd never dare say out loud. You may share the message before you place it in the bottle—or not. All the bottles will be released into the ocean to travel around the world and take your messages to each other with them."

Annie blinked. What would she never dare say out loud?

I'm crazy about you.

He probably knew that anyway.

Sinclair was frowning at his piece of paper. He glanced up at her with an odd look in his eyes. "Let's write something and not show each other."

"Okay." Anxiety fluttered in her stomach. What if he said they wouldn't look, then at the last minute they had to because of some party game? She picked up her pencil and chewed it thoughtfully. "At least they're not making us write rhyming couplets."

"True, though that might be fun." He paused for a moment, then started writing, looking intently at his paper.

She couldn't read the words, partly because a single candle on the table was their only light beyond the moon, and partly because his writing was worse than most doctors'. She turned to the blank square that sat mockingly on the table. A quick glance revealed that other guests at the tables around them were writing or even already squeezing their rolled-up papers into the neck of the bottle. "What if it ends up in the Great Pacific Plastic Patch?"

"What if it ends up in the hands of a lonely castaway on a remote Pacific island and gives him the strength to survive another month?"

"You apparently have a more romantic imagination than me." She snuck a glance at him. He'd rolled his paper into a thin cylinder, held between his thumb and finger. "And now I'm really curious about what you wrote."

He smiled mysteriously. "Maybe one day I'll tell you." His gaze lingered on her face for a moment, making heat rise under her skin.

Sinclair, I think you're a very handsome and thoughtful man who deserves to live happily ever after (preferably with me). She wrote the last part so tiny there was no way anyone could read it. *P.S. I love you.*

She rolled the message up fast and shoved it into the neck of the bottle before anyone could pry it from her fingers and make her read it aloud. Her hands trembled with the power of writing exactly what she wanted to, and not settling for saying the sensible thing. If it came back to haunt her someday, so what? Right now she was living a dream, if only for a night.

Did she really love him? She had no idea. Lack of experience again. She'd certainly never admired and adored a man as much as she did Sinclair. And a simple glance in her direction from him made her palms sweat. If that wasn't love it was something pretty close.

Sinclair pushed his message into the bottle and jammed in the cork their hosts had provided.

The waiter appeared again, and asked them to follow him. Annie rose from her chair, gathered her skirts, and she and Sinclair joined the other couples now walking across the broad sweep of lawn toward the Sound.

The moon cast an ethereal silver glow over the landscape. The lawn was a lush carpet underfoot and the slim beach at the shoreline glittered like crushed diamonds. Protected from the Atlantic by Long Island, the waveless water shimmered like a pool of mercury. Behind them the house resembled a fairy palace, its many windows lit and lanterns festooning the terraces.

As they grew closer she could see rowboats, almost like Venetian gondolas, lined up along a long, wooden dock. They bobbed slightly on the calm water. Attendants dressed in black brocade helped each couple into their own personal boat and gave the oars to the men, before pointing to a small, tree-cloaked island far out in the water.

"We're supposed to row out there in the dark?" Each gondola had a lantern, hung from a curlicue of wrought iron, at its stern.

"It'll be an adventure." Sinclair's low voice stirred something inside her. He took her hand, his skin warm and rough against hers. Her pulse quickened as they walked along the dock, amid laughs and shouts of mock distress from the other boaters. Sinclair and the staff helped her into the boat and seated her on a surprisingly comfortable plush seat, while Sinclair took up his place at the oar locks.

"Do stop at Peacock Island for refreshments." An elegantly attired man gestured toward the clump of trees dotted with lanterns, barely visible in the black night.

Sinclair pulled away from the dock with powerful

strokes, soon overtaking even the first boat to leave, and heading out into the quiet darkness of the sound.

Yet another bottle of champagne, beaded with tiny droplets of condensation, sat in a silver bucket at the prow of the boat. Annie resolved to keep her hands off it. Too much champagne might make her do something she would regret.

"The island is that way," she said, as he rowed swiftly past it, their wake lapping toward its shores.

"I know. I'm taking us somewhere else."

Eight

Sinclair enjoyed the pull of the oars in the heavy water. It felt good to move his muscles. The tension building between Annie and him all evening was beginning to tip from pleasurable to punishing.

Annie looked out over the side of the boat, staring at the long ribbon of the shore. The cool moonlight played across her features. He loved her face. She had a freshness about her that always caught his eye. Bright eyes, her mouth so quick to smile, that adorable nose with its faint sprinkling of freckles. Even in her extravagant gown and evening makeup she looked innocent and unworldly.

Was that what attracted him? Perhaps he was so jaded and tired of the world's movers and shakers that her quiet beauty and sweetness became irresistible.

Then there was her body. The voluminous skirt did nothing to hide his memory of her gorgeous, shapely legs...wrapped around his waist. The fitted bodice cupped her small, full breasts in a way that made his blood pump faster. Her gold-tinged hair was swept up into a knot, with a few strands escaping to play about her cheeks and momentarily hide her pretty blue eyes.

Was it really a good idea to take her to a private dock, away from the prying eyes of strangers? Probably not.

But he pulled away at the oars, as sure of his destination as he'd ever been.

"It's so quiet out here. I love it." Her voice drifted toward him, then she turned, all sparkling eyes and lush, full lips. "It's nice being away from the lights on the shore. We can see the stars." She looked up, and the moon glazed her face with its loving light.

Sinclair looked up, too, and almost startled at the bright mantle of stars—hundreds of them, millions—filling the dark sky above them. "I don't think I've looked up at the stars in years."

She laughed, a heartwarming sound. "And they've been up there all the time, shining away, waiting for you to remember them."

"I guess I've forgotten a lot of things. They say you get wiser as you get older, but I'm not so sure."

"We're not at the age where you get wiser yet. You have to go through other stages first, like the ones where you dream too big, then have your hopes crushed and get scared."

"What are you scared of?" She seemed so self-contained, in her neat domestic world, it was hard to imagine her being afraid of anything.

She shrugged, then hugged herself for a second. "Life not working out the way I hope it will. I think we're both in the phase of life where you start to realize it's now or never for a lot of things."

"You sound like my mom. She thinks if I don't have children this calendar year the Drummonds will vanish from the face of the earth and we'll both grow old and wizened alone together."

"I guess that's what she's scared of. I don't suppose you ever grow wise enough to stop worrying about some things. What are you afraid of?"

She fixed her steady blue gaze on him, expecting nothing less than the truth.

"Failure." He responded with honesty. "For all my success in business, I haven't succeeded where it matters most."

She looked at him, her eyes filled with understanding. "You want to have a family, and you're worried you never will."

"At this point I'm pretty sure I never will." She was so easy to talk to. He didn't feel the need to put on an impenetrable facade with her. "I've already tried twice and I know when to admit failure. If my marriage prospects were a publicly traded company I'd be dumping the stock." A smile crept to his mouth, despite his dismal confession. "Wouldn't you?"

"No." She hesitated, and a smile danced in her eyes. "But I'd be looking at how to enhance my business strategy for an increased chance of success. Perhaps a new approach to management, with more carefully selected principals."

He laughed. "You mean I need better taste in women."

She shrugged. Moonlight sparkled off her smooth skin. "Worth a try, at least."

Was Annie the right woman for him? The question hung in the still night air. No doubt she was wondering the same. No one sensible would recommend that a man of his background and position look for love with an "uneducated housekeeper"—but Annie was so much more than the sum of those two dismal words. What she lacked in formal education she'd obviously made up for with reading widely and observing closely. His previous marriages had proved that choosing a highly educated and ambitious mate was not necessarily a recipe for success.

"Where are we headed?"

Her question startled him. "I don't know. I only know that I enjoy your company immensely. And I think you're the sweetest, most beautiful woman I've ever met."

She stared for a moment, than laughed softly. "I appreciate your frank answer, but I meant, where are we rowing to? The lights from the party are totally out of sight."

"Don't worry. I know the Sound like the back of my hand. Rather better, in fact. Who really knows the back of their hand, anyway?" He smiled mysteriously.

"You still haven't answered my question." She tried to look stern, but a smile tugged at her lips. "Some people would be very nervous about being sailed off with in the dark with no idea where they're going."

"Are you nervous?"

"A little."

He wanted to reach out and reassure her, but couldn't take his hands off the oars. "We're going to the private dock of a friend of mine. I keep a boat there, in fact. It's just around this next headland." He gestured out into the darkness. You couldn't see anything now but dark, shimmering water and the broad cloak of stars over their heads, but he knew the curve of the coast like the face of an old friend.

At last the wooded shore beckoned, and he steered the boat into the familiar sheltered cove, where broad stone steps joined the water to the vast lawn of his friend's Victorian summer house. The house itself was shrouded in darkness, but moonlight illuminated the stone terraces with their sheltered seating areas. He docked the boat and tied it to one of the big, cast iron mooring rings. Annie giggled as he helped her to her feet so she could make a bold leap out of the boat, with her skirts gathered in one hand.

She glanced around. "I feel like we've landed at the Taj Mahal."

"I think that's what the architect intended. My friend's great-great-grandfather imported tea from India and wanted to recreate the pavilions of Assam here on Long Island." He led her through a stone archway to a row of cushioned seats that lined one side of the terrace.

"This should be more comfortable than the boat." He helped her sit down on the plush cushions. An ornately painted pavilion sheltered them from the moonlight, which filtered through the trees around them.

"I'm slightly worried that you brought me here to take advantage of me." She raised a slim brow.

"I brought you here so we could be alone together. That doesn't seem to be possible even in my own house right now."

"I think it's sweet the way you're taking care of your mom. They always say you can tell everything you need to know about a man by the way he treats his mother."

"Then maybe I'm not quite so dastardly as legend would have you believe."

She paused and looked at him. "I already know you're kind and thoughtful."

He laughed. "Maybe not as much as you think. It's possible that you have good reason to be worried for your virtue. Any man would be hard-pressed to resist the temptation of being alone in the dark with you."

In the privacy of the pavilion he let his hungry gaze roam over her, drinking in her soft skin, her gentle eyes, her lush, full mouth. Even her throat looked beautiful, and he fought the urge to kiss the curve of her neck, which sloped down to her pert, high breasts encased so enticingly in the silvery silk.

"As a woman, I have to admit I'm fighting my primal instincts to keep my hands off you, too." A mischievous smile danced in her eyes. "You look very hot in a tux."

He chuckled. "I can't encourage you to fight your instincts. I'm sure it's far healthier to indulge them."

"So you think I should give in to the urge to loosen your tie and collar?"

"I'm not sure if that's a good idea." A slow smile crept across his mouth. "But there's only one way to find out."

His muscles tightened as she reached up and tugged at one side of his silk bow tie. He could smell the subtle scent of her skin. He loved that she never wore perfume, and why would she? Her natural aroma was as intoxicating as the finest fragrance.

Her fingertips brushed his skin as she unbuttoned his collar, and sent a shiver of rich desire rolling through him. This really wasn't a good idea. He'd regretted sleeping with her the first time. It felt fantastic while they were writhing around on the bed together, but only moments later he was gripped by an agony of regret.

Why?

Right now he couldn't think of one good reason why he shouldn't be intimate with Annie Sullivan. They were both mature adults and in charge of their own destiny. He wasn't forcing her into anything. She seemed to be enjoying this as much as he was, if her dazzled expression was anything to go by.

And if he could gauge her desire by the way her mouth was moving slowly, but inexorably toward his...

Their lips met in a slow collision, like two thunderstorms meeting out over the ocean. Rain and hail and lightning exploded inside him at the touch of her skin to his. His hands flew out and gripped her with force, holding her close as he'd ached to for days.

Her hot breath on his skin set his senses on fire. Her fingers reached into his hair, down his neck, over his shirt, moving with fevered anxiety echoed in his own body. Before he could stop himself he'd undone some of the buttons on the back of her dress and slid his fingers inside. Instead of historical corsetry they met smooth, bare skin.

"Are you naked under this dress?"

"Maybe." He could hear the smile in her voice. "You'll have to explore to find out."

Her invitation tantalized him and worked like fresh oxygen on the flames of desire ripping through him. Undoing the buttons had loosened the shaped bodice, which softened its grip on her breasts.

Annie wasn't shy about undressing him. She pushed his jacket off and unbuttoned his shirt with an intent concentration that made him want to laugh. "You must be hot after all that rowing," she murmured as an excuse. The way she licked her lips, as if anticipating a treat, suggested a more delicious ulterior motive.

Already he was hard as the stone piers on the dock. The heat flushing his skin had more to do with anticipation than exertion. Having cracked open Annie's demure shell once—or did he simply peel it away?—he knew that a sensual and passionate woman lay beneath her quiet and compliant exterior.

She tugged his shirt from his pants with a flourish and pulled it off, exposing his chest and arms to the balmy night air. "Doesn't that feel better?"

"It does." He kissed her gently. "Especially because now I can do this." He pulled her closer, until her breasts spilled against the muscle of his chest, her taut nipples grazing his skin and shifting his arousal into high gear.

Their kiss deepened as they pressed against each other, skin to skin, surrounded by the whisper of trees and the gentle lapping of the water against the dock. For the first time in months—no, the second time—Sinclair felt a sense of peace and contentment well up inside him. Right here, right now, everything was perfect. Their kiss tasted like honey and fruit and champagne, tantalizing his taste buds and every other part of him.

Why did he feel this way with only Annie? He couldn't remember enjoying the company of a woman so much. Was it pure sexual attraction?

He didn't think so. There was something more substantial about the pleasure he felt in her company, but he couldn't put his finger on what it was.

He pulled back from their kiss, letting the night air cool his mouth before lowering it to her breasts. Her skin glowed in the silver moonlight, making her look like an ancient statue in a tempting state of undress. He licked her nipples, and enjoyed the little murmur of pleasure that escaped her lips. Her fingers roamed over the muscles of his back and arms, sparking little rivers of sensation that flowed through his body, and increasing the pressure building inside him like water behind a dam.

When Annie's hands slid inside the waistband of his pants he flinched, responding powerfully to the increased sensation. "I want to make love to you." It sounded so old-fashioned the way he said it, but he couldn't think of a better way to express his desires or intentions.

"And I want you to make love to me." She breathed it in his ear, hot and sultry. "Again."

His eyes slid closed as memories of their first encounter met and mingled with the sensations and emotions of the present. He fumbled with the last of the buttons on her dress and it fell and pooled around her feet before she stepped out of it, wearing nothing but a delicate pair of flesh-toned panties. She looked totally unselfconscious, a glorious, timeless study in feminine beauty, standing on the hand-hewn limestone of the terrace. The moon dressed her in light and shadow that emphasized the full curve of her breasts and the sweet pear shape of her behind. He could sit and stare at her for an hour.

But, growing impatient, and with a glint in her eye, she slid his belt out of the buckle and soon he was also naked in the moonlight.

"Are you sure we're alone here?" She glanced suddenly over her shoulder, into the dark woods on the edge of the lawn.

"There's probably a crowd of admirers in the trees." He let his fingers skate over the curve of her waist.

"You're kidding." Her eyes widened.

"But they'll keep our secrets. They have other things to do, like feather their nests, and bury their acorns in the tree trunks."

Her look of alarm mellowed into a smile. Then her expression grew more serious. "Is this going to be another secret?"

Her gaze hinted at a well of sadness beneath her lovely exterior. Guilt stabbed him for the way he'd pushed her aside after their surprise encounter. He'd been shocked at his own behavior. He was barely even divorced and already he'd pulled another woman into his bed. His emotions had been jolted out of the deep freeze and he didn't know how he felt about anything. His first and only impulse had been to run and keep on running.

But all that running had led him right back here into Annie's welcoming arms. "Only if you want it to be."

She looked at him, her eyes clear and bright. "I don't like secrets."

"Me, either. Usually they make me worry about the SEC and insider trading accusations." He watched the smile creep back onto her face. "But in this case it just seems unnecessary. We're adults."

"There's no arguing with that." She surveyed his body with a mischievous twinkle in her eye. "You're certainly all man."

His arousal pulsed stronger. His hands rested at her waist, and he pulled her gently to him and kissed her lips. "And you're all woman." He sighed as he ran his hands over the sweet curve of her backside. His erection pressed gently against the soft skin of her stomach, and throbbed with anticipation at finding an even more inviting and intimate hiding place.

Annie spread herself out on the elegant fabric, sheltered from the stars by an elaborate canopy. Her body looked like an invitation to sin, of the most enjoyable kind. Right now he must be the luckiest man alive.

Then a dark thought crossed his mind. "Now is probably not the ideal time to mention this, but I don't have a condom."

"Better now than afterwards." She simply smiled and shifted herself into an even more delectable pose. "But don't worry. I still have it covered."

Thank heaven. He wasn't sure if even a bracing plunge in Long Island Sound could take the edge off his current state of erotic tension. "That doesn't surprise me, since you're always prepared for everything."

He climbed over her on the wide, cushioned sofa, sinking against her warm skin and drinking in her subtle fragrance. Her arms wrapped around his back, holding him close as she layered kisses over his face. He sighed at the luxurious sensation of her body in his arms, and the ever growing ache inside him so close to being soothed.

Being with Annie felt utterly different from any encounter in his life before and he really had no idea why. Naturally a thinker, he'd usually be able to puzzle it out, but right now he didn't want to think at all. It was enough to just feel—in his body and in his heart.

He entered her slowly, kissing her inviting mouth. They moved together in a hypnotic rhythm, her soft sighs music that made his heart fill with joy. He loved the sensation of her hands on his body, even her nails digging into his flesh as the fever of their passion gripped her.

Lithe and agile, she moved with him on the lush, upholstered sofa. Astride him, she took him to new heights of agonized pleasure. Just when he thought he couldn't stand another second without exploding, she pulled back, a sly smile on her face, and shifted so that he was on top of her again.

He managed to roll over without losing his safe place deep inside her. Every inch of his body, every muscle and corpuscle, throbbed with intensity. Half of him wanted to climax and end the delicious agony, the other half wanted it to continue forever. To keep them both suspended in a blissful half-life of sensual pleasure.

Would they both regret this in the morning, when the champagne would wear off and the silver moonlight be replaced by blinding rays of harsh sun?

"I won't regret this."

Her rasped words startled him. She'd spoken as if she could read his thoughts. "I won't, either."

"Whatever happens next, we'll always have this moment." With her legs wrapped around his waist and her arms tight around his neck, Annie held him with force. The heat of her arousal, compounded with his own, threatened to make sparks in the air. "And I won't forget it."

A threat or a promise, her words drove him those last few miles out into the realm where worldly cares and concerns evaporated and there was nothing but right now. They shared a climax so forceful it almost threw them onto the stone terrace, and he had to brace with his arms to keep them on the cushions.

Panting, gasping and holding on for dear life, they

floated back down to earth together, chests heaving against each other.

"Why does that feel so good?" Annie's question, after a long silence, made him laugh.

"Because if it didn't there wouldn't be any people on earth. If having sex was like brushing your teeth people wouldn't bother."

"You don't brush your teeth?" Her eyes sparkled with both passion and humor.

"I'm the kind of person who does stuff out of a sense of duty."

"I like that about you."

"I can tell. You're the same. I bet you never go to bed without brushing your teeth."

"Am I that easy to read?" She pouted, or tried to, despite the smile tugging at her mouth.

"Yes, you're an open book."

Her smile faded slightly and a thoughtful look darkened her gaze. "Am I really? Did you know all along that I've...had a thing for you?"

He didn't know that. It hadn't crossed his mind that she felt that way about him. She'd simply been an excellent employee to him. How did you say that without sounding rude? "Something rendered me blind to your charms until our trip up to the attic. I don't know why, because you've been the same ravishing beauty—cunningly disguised by L.L. Bean—haunting my house for years."

She frowned slightly. "How odd that the trip up to the attic changed everything."

"My mom would say it's fate. Something mystical is happening." He spoke in a deliberately mysterious tone.

Annie glanced around, still holding tight to his body.

"I kind of feel that way, too. I'm not sure I would have ever dared to do...something like this before."

"Have hot, wild sex on a stranger's patio?"

"Pretty much. And with my boss, too. In fact I can't believe we're lying here naked under the moon."

"I know. There's a chill in the air." He pretended to hold her closer, like a blanket.

"Is there? I can't feel it. But then I'm glowing all over, thanks to you."

She *was* glowing. Her eyes, her skin, her whole spirit radiated joy, good health and happiness. And he had the power to increase or destroy that happiness.

A dark shadow crept across his heart. He didn't know how to keep a woman happy. He could make it past the wedding, past the honeymoon, and then, somehow, it all fell apart.

But maybe, with Annie, it could be different.

He jolted upright. Was he seriously thinking about embarking on another relationship so soon after the disastrous failure of his second marriage? And if he wasn't, what the heck was he doing here with this beautiful and sweet woman naked in his arms?

"What's the matter?" The concern in her voice wrung his soul.

"I'm not naturally suited to living in the present."

She stroked his cheek. Her serious expression didn't mock his doubts and worries. She seemed to silently accept them. "I usually live in the future. I go through the motions in the present, rinsing lettuce and making beds, but my mind and spirit are way ahead in 'one day' land."

He frowned. He was good at living on the edge and going with the flow in business, but his personal life was a whole other story. "I suspect I tend to lag behind in 'if only' territory."

"Then there's obviously no hope for us, is there?" She spoke brightly, but there was an undercurrent of sadness to her tone.

"Either that, or we'll have to save each other and only live in the present from now on." A fresh flame of hope—or was it simply desire—roared through him, and he took her mouth in a fierce kiss. She kissed him back hard, gripping him as if sheer strength and determination could hold them here, at least for a few moments longer.

When their lips finally parted he felt breathless and light-headed.

"I hate to live in the future as usual, but we'd better get back to the party before it ends or our driver will wonder what happened to us." Annie's soft voice tugged him back to the present.

"You're right." He stretched, easing against Annie's warm body. "Though it pains me to put clothes back on when I feel so comfortable without them."

"I like putting my dress back on. I never know what's going to happen when I put on one of the dresses from that trunk."

"Or maybe you do know what's going to happen now. There's a definite theme." He traced the line of her jaw with his thumb. Her lip quivered as he drew close. "Involving me taking the dresses off."

They put their clothes on and climbed—gingerly—into the boat. The journey back to the party seemed so much quicker than the trip out, maybe because of the way the current was flowing. Or maybe because he hated to see their evening together end. He had an unsettling feeling that everything would be different once they got back to the mundane world of other people and their cares.

Annie sat at the prow of the boat, looking out over the dark water, which was choppy now, rippled with undercurrents and invisible forces that broke up its formerly smooth surface.

"What's that?" She looked up suddenly at a bright light in the sky, rising like a comet behind the dark shadows of the woodland along the shore.

"It's a Chinese lantern. They're popular at parties now. You light the wick inside and the paper lantern floats up, and drifts in the sky until it finally burns up."

As they rounded the last bend in the river, the sky seemed to fill with lanterns, drifting higher and floating out into the night.

"They're beautiful." Annie watched, mesmerized. "But they seem so dangerous. They could touch down somewhere and start a fire."

The water all around them did nothing to cool the fire burning in his heart. This time was going to be different. His tryst with Annie would turn into a real relationship, and they'd figure out how to live together in a way that didn't cramp each other's style and threaten to turn them into different people. Maybe they'd even marry and have a family.

Sinclair drew in a deep, hard breath. He was getting carried away. Better just to pull on the oars and keep going, and let the future take care of itself.

"Do I look okay?" Annie turned to him as they drew nearer to the shore, fingers tucking her hair back into its bun.

"You look ravishing." She was even more beautiful

with the final polish gone from her dress and makeup. More natural and sexy. "I hope no one will realize that I've been ravishing you this whole time."

She gave him a seductive smile. "That will be our secret. I don't think anyone ever needs to know we were such rude guests." She gasped. "We never even went to the island!"

"Never mind. We'll tell them we got lost."

In a way, that was how he felt. He'd wandered off the usual course of his life, got lost in Annie, and found himself in a wondrous new land of possibilities.

"I can't wait to get lost again."

"Me, either." But he frowned. He couldn't shed the nagging doubt that this wild and perfect evening might be his last taste of paradise on earth.

You don't know how to live. His second wife's words echoed in his brain. *You're always worrying about your duties and responsibilities. You have no idea how to have fun.* She'd have been horrified to leave the "fun" of the party for the secret world of the waterfront pavilion. He suddenly wanted to laugh at the realization that he'd come to this party out of obligation. Much like the stupid croquet game he'd played to humor his mom and help her recovery. And she'd thrust Annie on him in her borrowed finery, knowing his sense of duty would make him take her to the party.

Sometimes a sense of duty could be a beautiful thing.

When they got home, Annie immediately crept back to her bedroom like one of the twelve dancing princesses. If this affair with Sinclair was about to turn into a real relationship, then everyone would know about it sooner or later, but four in the morning was not the best time to declare their newfound passion.

She frowned. Why did the princesses in the fairy tale have to be so secretive and sneak off to their princes every night? Why couldn't they just marry them and live happily ever after? She didn't remember ever seeing a good explanation for that in the story. Maybe they weren't princesses at all, but housekeepers who had to get up early and scrub the floors before dawn, and who'd be in trouble if anyone found out they were skimping on sleep while wearing out their shoes.

Sinclair had made the evening so perfect. From the moment he'd been surprised with her as his partner for the evening, he'd been romantic, charming and adorable. He'd treated her like a princess and made her fall even more hopelessly in love with him.

When they stepped out of their accustomed roles, he was so easy to talk to, and so much more interesting than the men she'd been on dates with. He seemed to know at least a little about everything under the sun, which allowed her to stretch her own mind. She tried her best to fill in the gaps in her education by devouring books and magazines on every subject, and it was fun to realize that he'd acquired a lot of his knowledge the same way. Maybe they weren't so different after all?

Annie smiled as she read a message she found on her pillow: *Don't you dare get up until noon!* Katherine Drummond had signed it *Kate* in an intimate flourish. She set the piece of monogrammed notepaper on the nightstand with a sigh and slid beneath her covers. Sinclair unleashed something absolutely wild inside her, and filled her with hope for a future she'd never dared to reach for. Would they tell everyone tomorrow at breakfast? Would he pledge his undying love for her in front of his mom and Vicki over her handmade omelets?

She couldn't help a strange, nagging feeling that something entirely different would happen.

Nine

Annie came very close to obeying the command in Katherine's note. Though she'd set her alarm for seven, she had no recollection of switching it off when she finally woke again near eleven-thirty.

She sat upright. Had she really made love with Sinclair again last night? It grew hard to separate dreams from reality lately. Or nightmares. What kind of crazy person slept with her boss for no good reason other than that he was gorgeous and she couldn't resist him?

The champagne was at least partly to blame, but what happened to her self-control when she was alone with him? She groaned. She could remember word for word the intimate and romantic conversations they'd had afterward, but now their sentiments seemed fanciful. The kind of thing that sounds perfectly reasonable by moonlight but silly in the cold light of day.

I won't regret this. She'd said it then, and believed it

completely. But now, as she lowered her feet onto the cold wood floor and pondered how he'd react when he saw her, she wasn't so sure.

She showered and dressed, wondering what everyone had eaten for breakfast. At least now she could busy herself with lunch and stay hidden in the kitchen for a while. Heart thudding, she let herself out of her room and walked quickly down the corridor.

"Back in your khakis already." Vicki's voice made her jump. She turned to see Vicki marching along the hall behind her brandishing a newspaper. "What would the editors at *Women's Wear Daily* think?"

"I doubt they'd have any thoughts on the subject." She tried to sound casual yet polite, and it came out sounding forced. *Women's Wear Daily* was just one of several papers that filled the mailbox since Vicki's arrival.

"Ah, but that's where you're wrong." Vicki swept past her into the kitchen and spread the paper out on the kitchen island.

Annie froze at the sight of a double-page spread with three huge pictures of her at the dance last night. "What?" She squinted at them. The headline jumped out at her. "Mystery Woman in Mystery Dress." "Why would they print this?"

"Because you had everyone talking last night." She crossed her arms and looked triumphant. "And apparently you and Sinclair missed dinner."

Dinner? She hadn't even noticed that they never ate it. They went right from oysters to… She could see how the aphrodisiac rumors got started.

"This being the fashion press, they're even more

curious about who designed your gown than who was in it."

"Whoever designed it is long dead." Annie moved closer, increasingly fascinated by the pictures. One showed her dancing with Sinclair, his arms around her waist and her skirt in a whirl that showed how big the skirt was, even without a crinoline. Another showed them walking across the terrace. Then there was a three-quarter picture showing Sinclair with his arm around her waist, which seemed poured into the fitted gown.

"They don't know that. They're thinking it's by the next Balenciaga." She laughed loudly. "This is the most fun I've had in months!"

"Where's Sinclair?" She said it softly. Had he seen these pictures that boldly proclaimed their romantic liaison to the world?

"He's been on the phone most of the morning. Work, I suppose. He's such a stick-in-the-mud. But it looks like you shook him loose last night. He's almost radiant in that last picture."

Annie's breath caught as she saw the expression on his face. A close-up of them dancing, her dress floating out behind her and her arms on his shoulders. And an expression of…rapture on his handsome face.

"We had a really good time." She said it so quietly that it sounded eerie, like an apology.

"I can see that." Vicki grabbed a glass from a shelf and filled it with iced water from the dispenser on the fridge. "Exactly as I intended."

"You faked the headache, didn't you?"

She laughed. "I'm a martyr to them, and don't you tell anyone otherwise. You needed to go to that ball, young lady. I *had* a ball waving my magic wand over you, and look how well it turned out." She beamed with such obvious good cheer that Annie almost began to like her. "And this won't be the last of it. I bet you're on Page Six as well. You'll be the talk of all New York."

Annie blinked. How would Sinclair react to all this? Like the old-school aristocrat he was, he seemed skilled at avoiding publicity, despite his illustrious career and many high-profile friends. She'd searched online for him more than once, when he hadn't visited the house in a while and she just felt like seeing his face. A few photos from parties and a corporate portrait were all she found. She didn't imagine he'd be happy to see these pictures plastered all over the papers.

Especially once they figured out that the woman in his arms was his own housekeeper. "Sinclair is going to be upset."

"Who cares? He needs to live a little. And I think the two of you make an adorable couple." She tapped the picture of them dancing. "Tell me that isn't romantic."

Annie's heart squeezed at the image of herself and Sinclair, staring intently at each other as they whirled around the dance floor as if no one else existed and the music was being played only for them. Last night they had found their own little world together, and inhabited it so fully they forgot about the consequences.

"I hope he won't be embarrassed." She chewed her nail absently for a moment, then pulled her hand back. "I think we both got carried away by the atmosphere of the evening."

"Good. Sinclair needs to get carried away more often. I'll make sure his mom and I are out late to-night." She gave Annie a knowing look and swept out of the room, leaving the pages open on the island. Annie quickly closed the paper and tucked it out of sight in the pantry. She didn't want anyone—especially Sinclair—to come in and think she'd been gloating over it.

Heavy footfalls on the stairs made her hands shake as she shredded chicken into a salad. Given that Katherine and Vicki were both built and moved like gazelles, it could be only one person. Heart bumping, she quickly dried her hands and tucked a stray lock of hair into her bun.

Last night had been so magical, so breathtaking. It was a dream come true in every sense of the word, and even the pictures in the paper had captured that. Would electricity jump between them as he entered the room? She felt her temperature rise, and started to take off her light sweater when he entered the doorway. How should she greet him? With a cheery hello? Maybe even a kiss…?

His expression stopped her cold. The angles of his chiseled face looked harder than she'd ever seen them. He filled the door frame, all broad shoulders and hard planes. His onyx gaze met hers with the force of a blow.

She swallowed. Her romantic fantasies shriveled up and went to hide under the island. "I had a really nice time last night." She was going to say how she felt, damn it, and not let mystery and suspense rule the air. She wasn't going to let him sweep their fantasy evening under the rug this time. If nothing else, they'd at least talk about it. "But I'm guessing you don't feel the same."

He shoved a hand through his hair. It looked as if he'd done that a few times already. "Annie." He came into the kitchen and closed the door. Which could have been an intimate gesture, but his tense physique and stony expression made it unsettling instead. He hesitated, as if searching his brain for what to say.

"Don't tell me to forget last night happened. I won't do it again." She heard the tone of desperation in her own voice. "I can't." She gripped her sweater in her fist, digging her nails into the fabric.

"Last night was…" His broad brow furrowed. "It was wonderful." He met her gaze, and the pain in his dark eyes rooted her to the spot.

"Then why do you look so unhappy?" Part of her wanted to rush to him and throw her arms around him. The other, more experienced and sensible part, wanted to wrap her arms around herself and shield her heart from whatever was coming.

"Something's happened."

"Is it your mom?" Panic rushed her. She hadn't seen Katherine yet, and had just assumed she was up and out of the house already. "What's wrong?"

"Not my mom." His frown deepened. "My ex-wife, Diana."

She blinked. He hadn't even spoken to her in months, as far as she knew. They'd had an acrimonious divorce, with lawyers and angry words, despite the short duration of their marriage. "Is she ill?"

"No." He inhaled and blew it out. "She's pregnant."

"Oh." The word fell from Annie's lips as her heart sank a full inch in her chest. "And it's yours." Why else would it be such a big deal?

"Yes. She's due to give birth any day now. She said she didn't want to tell me, since our marriage was ending, but now that she's drawing close to delivery she felt the need to tell the truth."

Or the need to apply for child support. Annie kept

her unkind thought to herself. But she couldn't help saying another. "Hasn't she been involved with someone else?" The gossip was that his wife had cheated on him. She didn't know the whole story. "Couldn't it be the other man's baby?" She braced herself for Sinclair's reaction. It wasn't a kind thing to suggest.

"I just spoke to her on the phone. She swears the story was just an excuse for the divorce, and that the baby is mine."

"She wants to reconcile?" She couldn't help doubt creeping into her voice.

Sinclair's pained expression gave her the answer. "No, she doesn't. But she's due any day now. If it is my baby, I need to be there for the birth."

A tiny flame of hope leaped in her chest at the word *if.* Obviously he wasn't entirely sure the child was his.

"Why didn't she tell you before now, if she's so far along?"

Sinclair frowned. "She said she didn't want me to know about it." The hurt in his eyes stole her breath. "That she wanted to raise it on her own."

Frustration rose in Annie's craw. "So why don't you let her do that?"

"I'd never forgive myself if our child grew up in a broken family without me making every effort to fix it."

"You don't have to marry her again to make it okay. Plenty of people live in separate households and play a full role in raising their children." Was he really going to walk away from her after all their declarations of last night?

"I know. But it's who I am, I suppose." That inscrutable dark gaze met hers. "I have to try."

"I understand." Of course he'd want to do the "right

thing" and be an old-fashioned *Leave It to Beaver* dad. He was hardly the type to feel fulfilled by taking the kids out for pizza and a movie twice a month. "I hope it all works out." That last part was a lie. But maybe in time she'd have the generosity of spirit to truly wish that for him. Right now she wanted to curl into a ball and sob.

Sinclair shoved a hand through his hair. "I just got off the phone with her. She's living in Santa Barbara right now. I'm going to fly there this afternoon."

"Oh." So much for their evening of romance tonight, with Vicki whisking Katherine away. Annie cursed herself for the selfish thought. Sinclair's life would be thrown into turmoil by this, no matter what happened.

And her own life?

No one cared about that very much.

"I'm so sorry this had to happen, especially now." Sinclair looked genuinely agitated. "I'd never have... taken advantage of you again last night if I'd had any idea."

His words cut her like a dagger. "You didn't take advantage of me." She tried to keep her voice cool. "I was a willing participant." *More fool, me.* Then again, it wasn't his fault this had happened. Or was it? He didn't have to rush to his ex-wife's side and try to rekindle their romance. He could just as easily have explained it all, then given her a big romantic kiss.

But life didn't work like that. At least, hers didn't. She pulled the paper out of the pantry. "Did you see this?" She flipped to the double-page spread of their romantic evening.

Sinclair snatched it from her. "Damn."

Annie shriveled a little bit more. "I didn't notice them

taking the pictures." She was too wrapped up in their oh-so-temporary romance.

"Me, either." He flipped to the front cover. "What kind of paper is this, anyway?"

"It's a fashion thing. Vicki gave it to me. She gets a copy every day."

"She would." He put it down, folded so their pictures were hidden. "Let's hope the story doesn't leak to the mainstream press."

"Yeah." It was hard to even speak. He really did want to sweep their glorious evening under the rug. Pain welled up inside her. She could only pray that he'd leave before it spilled out as tears.

"I'll go pack. Don't bother making me lunch. I'm leaving for the airport in ten minutes."

Already they were back to a business relationship. She nodded, keeping her mouth shut tight. Inside she was slowly dying.

"I'm sorry, Annie." His voice was gruff, a little stiff. She wasn't sure whether he was trying to put on a brave front or whether he simply didn't feel anything. She was beginning to suspect the latter.

"Me, too." She folded the paper and put it back into the pantry, glad to get away from that cold, dark stare. When she turned back, he was gone.

She leaned on the island, trying to catch her breath after holding in her emotions so tightly. She wanted to scream, to cry out in pain and frustration. But she didn't. She'd dared to live the dream for one beautiful night. She should be proud of herself for being bold and brave enough to live life to the fullest. Expecting more was just greedy.

She took her sweet time making the salad, anxious

to be sure Sinclair was gone before she ventured out of the kitchen to set the table or call the others to lunch.

"Oh, crap." Vicki's voice made her jump so violently she spilled some of the sea salt she was sprinkling on the garlic bread. "Sinclair blows it again."

Annie shrugged. Didn't turn around. She didn't want Vicki to know how hurt she was. She didn't understand at all why Vicki kept trying to push her and Sinclair together. Right now she felt like a mouse that had been played with too hard and long by a cat. She wasn't in the mood to provide any more entertainment.

"It's bad luck. Sinclair looks like he's seen a ghost."

"Has he left yet?" Annie glanced out the window. She couldn't see his car from here.

"Just drove out of here like he had a hellhound on his heels."

She finally turned to look at Vicki. "Why does he want to reconcile when his ex-wife doesn't?" The question burned in her brain. She didn't know what kind of relationship they had. Though if Diana had gone through almost an entire pregnancy without telling him, they could hardly be close.

"Sinclair is a diehard romantic. He probably believes a baby can fix everything. Diana isn't, though. She's about as emotional as this radish." She plucked a radish from the bunch on the counter, and bit into it.

Annie's heart was breaking. It seemed such a waste. She and Sinclair could have been happy together, but now he was going back to a woman who'd only hurt him.

"Why did Sinclair fall in love with her?" It felt good to get the question off her chest.

Vicki shrugged. "She's beautiful. Very manipulative and controlling. She probably told him what he wanted to hear." She raised a brow. "At least until after they were married."

"Why wouldn't she tell him she was pregnant until now?"

"I suppose it didn't suit her. Maybe she had someone even richer and more handsome up her sleeve." She shook her head. "Though frankly that's hard to imagine. Sinclair's a real catch."

"Then how come you don't want him for yourself?" Annie could hardly believe how bold and blunt she was being. Maybe because she had nothing left to lose. "I can tell that you don't."

Vicki laughed. "Sinclair's far too good for me. He'd be thoroughly wasted." Her violet eyes took on a wistful look. "Sinclair really is one in a million, and I don't say that because of his wealth and flashy looks. He's a truly good person, principled to the core, who only wants to do the right thing."

"So how come he keeps screwing up?"

Vicki stared at her for a moment, then snorted with loud laughter. "You're showing a whole other side of yourself today, Annie. And your guess is as good as mine. Why are men stupid? It's the eternal question of women."

Annie rankled at Vicki calling Sinclair stupid. He was as intelligent as a person could get. On the other hand, he had very poor taste in women. Except for her. Or was she just another example of him falling into the arms of someone utterly wrong for him?

Her insides felt raw and empty and her brain worked too hard to grapple with events that didn't make any sense at all. Poor Sinclair, doomed to make the same mistake again. And poor her, left alone to lick her wounds.

Vicki played with the clasp on her heavy silver bracelet. "Oh, well. He's gone now. All good things must come to an end, though this certainly wasn't the end I had in mind. I'm sorry for encouraging you." The look she shot her was genuinely apologetic. "I hope I haven't screwed things up for you."

"Not any more than they already were." Annie let out a sigh. She couldn't stay now. There was no way she could continue to work here after making love to Sinclair for a second time and being unceremoniously dumped again. It didn't matter how good his reason was, she needed to save herself from this situation. That would mean leaving Katherine Drummond in the lurch, but she could hire someone else to buy her fresh greens and bake quinoa muffins for the rest of the summer. "I'd better put lunch out."

"I'll bring the plates."

Lunch was a grim affair. Annie wasn't sitting at the table, of course, but hovering nearby. Katherine, usually talkative and full of plans, was oddly silent. She looked paler than she had lately. Apparently the news of her new grandchild was not quite as happy as it could have been. "Oh, poor Sinclair," she said at last, after toying with her chicken salad for a while. "That woman will never make him happy."

"She won't." Vicki was the only one with an appetite. She helped herself to more salad and bread. "So we'll have to hurry up and put this damn cup back together and get the fates back on the right track."

Katherine gave a small laugh. "I'm beginning to think it's just a story and that there's no cup at all.

We've been through nearly every box and basket and strange multi-strapped valise in that attic. We've certainly found some interesting things, but nothing that looks like one-third of a three-hundred-year-old Scottish cup."

Vicki lacked her usual sparkle. "Maybe the three brothers reunited and put it back together, and this is as good as it gets."

"They didn't, though." Katherine frowned at her untouched glass of sparkling water. "Aaron Drummond, the son of our ancestor, kept a diary and he wrote several times about his father's disappointment at never reuniting with his brothers. He was moaning about it on his deathbed."

"Bummer. Why didn't they get back together?"

"According to his diary, one of the brothers was arrested for stealing, escaped from prison and became a pirate, harassing vessels from Virginia to Florida. Then he disappeared. The third brother made his fortune trapping beavers, then went back to Scotland and bought back the ancestral home. They're still there. I suppose an Atlantic crossing wasn't the kind of journey you'd make just to visit family, back then. So they never even saw each other again. Our ancestor built the oldest part of this house, and our branch of the family has owned it ever since, so if his piece of the cup is anywhere at all, it's here."

"And maybe it will stay here for another three hundred years." Vicki sighed and broke off a piece of bread. "As for reuniting all three pieces, I don't imagine the pirate ancestor took very good care of his piece, anyway."

"According to contemporary stories he had gold and treasure buried all up and down the East Coast. Not here, though. He never came near New York. Maybe he didn't want to face his brother after he became an outlaw." She stared at her glass for a moment.

"It would be interesting to at least get the other relatives searching for the other pieces. Maybe you could offer a reward to sweeten the pot?"

"A reward? As far as I know, the other Drummond descendants are as wealthy as Sinclair. They'd hardly go digging up the garden for a few grand."

"Exactly." Vicki leaned forward. "They don't care about it because they think they have everything they need already. It might make more sense to get other people involved. Someone with a true financial incentive will hunt for the cup to earn the money, then the Drummonds will benefit from their hard work."

"Total strangers?" Katherine looked alarmed.

"It's an idea. Otherwise I'm worried we'll never find all three pieces."

From her vantage point near the sideboard, Annie noticed that calculating look creep back into Vicki's eyes. She wandered back into the kitchen. She couldn't care less about Vicki's nefarious plots at this point. She just needed to get lunch over with and give notice. Right now she felt numb as a zombie. She was about to quit her job of six years, had no place to go except the home—admittedly loving—she'd tried so hard to escape, and no prospect of any job at all.

"You're not going to quit, are you?" Vicki's voice sounded right next to her in the kitchen. How did this woman move around like a shadow?

"Why do you care?" Her emotions bubbled into her voice. "What does it matter? I'm sure you think I'm wasting my life dusting the sideboards here, anyway."

"Well, that is true." Vicki frowned. "I guess I just don't want it to be my fault."

"Trust me. It isn't. I've been thinking about moving on with my life and this is the final kick in the pants I needed, so you can enjoy the rest of the summer guilt-free. Though I would appreciate it if you looked out for Katherine. I promised Sinclair I'd take care of her, but…" Her chest tightened at the prospect of letting him down. She didn't like to go back on her word. On the other hand, it was time she put herself first for once. She'd been a doormat for too long, and these people were all adults who could take care of themselves, or at least pay someone else handsomely to do it.

"Of course." Vicki looked totally serious. "I'll make sure she has the most relaxing and healthful summer of her life." She exhaled. "What a mess. I hope Sinclair doesn't do anything really stupid, like marry Diana again."

"Whatever he does, it's none of my business. Now if you'll excuse me, I need to speak with Katherine."

Ten

Sinclair pulled his rented car out of the Santa Barbara airport with a drumbeat of dread in his heart. He didn't relish the sight of his ex-wife's face. He'd learned, gradually, that its perfect contours and smooth skin were not the result of a peaceful temperament or even good breeding, but rather the skill and tenacity of an army of surgeons and technicians with expertise in everything from sandblasting to spray tans. Terrified of wrinkles, she slept with a paste of cream around her eyes and neck. Even her lustrous dark hair wasn't natural. She had hanks of someone else's hair woven into it every three weeks. A bitter taste rose in his mouth at the prospect of ever having to kiss those silicone-plumped lips again.

Pain stabbed his heart at the memory of Annie's natural beauty. Her pale skin with its light sprinkling of freckles over her nose and cheeks. Her hair, which at first appeared to be light brown, but in a shaft of light revealed itself as a mass of red-gold silk. Her natural features, so pretty in their slight unevenness, and the crinkles that danced around her eyes when she smiled. Her slender, natural body with its ripe, soft curves and eager affection.

Regret soaked through him at the memory of how he'd treated her. Hungry with need that had clawed at his insides for two weeks, he'd peeled her beautiful dress off her and ravished her under the moonlight, with barely a sprinkling of pleasantries to smooth the way. He'd never felt such powerful desire for any woman and he still didn't understand it. Something about Annie reached deep inside him and held on tight.

So to have to tell her, this morning, that they couldn't be together, was agonizing. Cruel to her, torture for him. He let out a curse. Frustration crackled in his veins. He'd come so close to what seemed like happiness, only to have it snatched away again.

Maybe he was cursed. His mom was right and the whole damn family line was doomed to a miserable existence in a marriage of quiet resentment, like the one he'd witnessed between his own parents.

The cold grip of dread grew stronger as he pulled up in front of Diana's house. It seemed only a few months ago that they'd chosen it—well, she had, he hadn't liked the ornate Mediterranean exterior much, but at that point he was still trying to make his new bride happy. He'd been glad to give it to her in the divorce and say goodbye to both at the same time.

Muscles taut, he rang the doorbell. No answer. He rang again. Three cars sat in the driveway, so someone was home. At last he heard footsteps on the stone-tiled hallway and the door was flung open. "Sinclair!" The alarmed tone and the appalled look on his ex-wife's face gave him all the welcome he'd been expecting.

"I had to come see you."

"Why? I told you not to come." She made no move to invite him in. She filled the doorway almost completely, her huge belly hidden behind a veritable toga of ivory silk. Her face was bloated and puffy, which, combined with her heavy makeup, made her look like something from a horror movie.

Stop these ugly thoughts. She's the mother of your child.

"Why? Because we're having a child together."

"No, we're not." She glanced behind her. He thought he saw someone move in the large kitchen at the far end of the foyer. "*I'm* having a baby. We're divorced, in case you've forgotten. Still, since you're here, you better come in."

Her voice had an acid tone he hadn't heard before. Maybe now the divorce was final she didn't feel the need to cajole him into giving her more of what she loved most—money.

"If I'm the father…" Yes, he had doubts. But those weren't enough to keep him away. An innocent baby deserved the benefit of the doubt. "Then I intend to play a full and active role in our child's life, and we'll need to establish at the very least an honest working relationship." Any ideas of getting back together with her had fled at the sight of her angry, bitter stare.

"What's up, babe?" A gruff male voice echoed from the back of the house.

She swallowed and glanced behind her again.

"Who's that?" Sinclair's hackles rose. Was she living with someone already? Right now the thought of another man raising his child made his chest hurt.

"That's Larry. Larry, come meet Sinclair." She regarded him coolly as a hulking brute of a man, aged about twenty-two and with bleached blond hair, appeared behind her.

Larry nodded and took up a bodyguard-like position behind Diana.

"May I come in?" It rankled having to ask for an invitation into the house he'd bought for them to share.

"I suppose you'll have to." Diana turned, caftan flaring, and walked along the highway to an overdecorated living room. "Though you won't need to stay long. I told you our marriage is over."

"Not if we're having a child together. Why didn't you mention the pregnancy during the divorce?"

She twisted a big ring on one of her fingers. "I didn't want you feeling like you owned a part of me." She lifted her proud chin. "That you had rights over my future."

"Then why now?" None of this made sense.

She gestured to her large belly. "My livelihood depends on me being able to attend parties and interface with people. I confess I didn't realize how much a pregnancy would impact that. Obviously I can't be seen in public right now."

He wanted to laugh—or at the very least, agree. Instead he just felt sad. "So this is all about money. You don't want me in your child's life—you just want me to bankroll your existence while you take care of it."

"Pretty much." Her hard stare made his chest constrict.

"Have you taken a DNA test?"

"Yes, I told you that on the phone."

It was the reason he'd come here so fast. But now that he was here, something about the situation smelled like a week-dead New York City subway rat. "Let me see the results."

"I don't know where they are." She crossed her arms in the valley between her swollen breasts and her enormous belly.

"So you just expect me to take your word for it that they show the baby is mine?"

"I know you don't want a messy court case. And really, a little child support is peanuts to you. Just pay it and leave me alone. I'll let you see the child whenever you want."

Something in her eyes made him want to push further. "I need to see the test results." Diana wasn't a liar. If anything she was honest to a fault. There must be a reason she wouldn't show him the results.

"You do not. I'm nine months pregnant. Nine months ago we were still married," she snarled angrily. "The baby's yours. Do the math."

"That assumes that you weren't cheating on me during our marriage, when you've already admitted that you were."

"I only said that because New York doesn't have no-fault divorce, so somebody has to cheat." That's what she'd claimed at the time. He hadn't believed her then, either. "I conceived while still married, and you're the father."

"I no longer intend to take your word for anything. You'll have to take another test."

"I'm not putting the baby at risk by having a needle stabbed into my womb at this late stage." Her eyes bulged as she stared at him, and her swollen breasts looked as if they might pop right out of her toga. Which was not an appetizing thought.

"Then I'll wait here until it's delivered. One of the advantages of owning your own company is that you can do as you please, and from the look of you, I won't have to wait here long." If it was his baby he'd swallow his resentment and anger and make the best of the situation. If it wasn't...?

"Annie!" Her grandmother's big, soft arms encased her in a hug that made her want to collapse and rest. "Why've you been a stranger so long?"

"I was home for Christmas." That sounded pathetic. "I've just been wrapped up in...stuff." She'd quit her job in Dog Harbor yesterday and left early this morning, with most of her belongings in cardboard boxes that had been very awkward to carry on the train.

"How long are you staying?" Her grandmother pushed her back so she could survey her. "You look pale as a slab of squid. You're not sick, are you?"

She shook her head and tried to smile. "I'm fine." Just heartsick. "I'd like to stay until I find a new job. If you'll all have me back, that is."

Granny Pat's mouth opened wide for a moment. "You quit your job?"

She nodded. "It was time. I'd been there six years and was stuck in a rut."

Her grandmother grimaced. "Not a great time to find a job, hon. Your sister's been looking with no luck."

"I know. But I couldn't help it." She tried for a casual shrug.

"Something else is wrong." Her grandma's pale blue eyes narrowed. "I can always tell."

"There was...someone." Tears welled up inside her and she willed them not to spill from her eyes. "But that's over now." Thankfully the story had never moved into the mainstream process.

"Oh." Granny Pat folded her arms to her ample bosom again. "Poor baby. You tell Granny Pat where he lives and I'll go shake some sense into him."

Annie had to laugh. "If only it were that easy."

"Well, come in and park your stuff. We've been piling junk in your old room, but we'll move it out on the double."

The junk didn't have anywhere else to go, though, so that night she found herself in bed surrounded by grocery boxes full of garage-sale "treasures" that her mom and grandma had accumulated over the past few years. Maybe if she looked through them hard enough she'd find one-third of an old Scottish cup. Her bed was lumpy, and single. Being back in it felt like the grimmest admission of failure.

Sinclair was probably back between the sheets with the dreaded Diana, eagerly awaiting the arrival of his firstborn. She stared up at the ceiling, where cobwebs had formed around the 1970s light fixture, and tried not to miss her peaceful bedroom back in Dog Harbor, with the trees rustling outside and the call of owls in the early morning. That was all in the past and it was up to her to make her own future now. Tomorrow she'd enroll for fall courses at the community college. She had ample savings that she'd been piling up to build her little dream house, and she could live on them for some time, even if it meant eating her own dream for a while.

She really didn't want to know what was going on with Sinclair and his ex. He'd flown back to her without a moment's hesitation, which plainly showed how shallow and insignificant any feelings he had for Annie truly were. After all, he freely admitted to barely noticing her until she put the Victorian dress on. What he felt for her was obviously no more than temporary lust, easily forgotten once the heat of the moment wore off.

The mattress springs screeched as she climbed out of her bed. Sunlight poured unceremoniously through the ugly nylon curtains with their garish flowers. She'd grown used to the subtle and textured décor of the very rich, and now she'd probably be cursed with expensive tastes for the rest of her life.

She wasn't going to sit around waiting for life to happen. She splashed water on her face at the sink and patted her skin dry. She was going to make it happen. Maybe she wouldn't take the world by storm like the kind of women Sinclair was attracted to, but she'd forge her own dreams into reality, one little bit at a time.

"Do we get any of those dreamy eggs you're so good at?" Her dad's voice boomed up the stairs. She laughed. No chance of a day off here. Unlike Sinclair's house, where she was alone much of the time, she'd have a constant source of "clients" for her well-honed culinary skills. At least that would give her something useful to do, instead of hanging around moping in her old room.

"Coming!" She dressed quickly and went downstairs, but when she got to the kitchen, no one was around. They'd show up soon enough once cooking smells filled the air. She cracked some eggs into a bowl and heated the pan, then peeled some strips of bacon off the big slab from the butcher and put them in to sizzle.

Sinclair didn't like bacon, and she'd gone off it, too, since living in his house. Which was all the more reason to start eating it again.

You came here to leave Sinclair behind and move on. She slapped the cooked bacon onto a plate and tipped eggs into the hot pan. Sinclair would never eat eggs fried in bacon grease.

Why was she still thinking about him? Frustration made her growl aloud, and she racked her brain for something else to focus on. She should think about her future. What kind of job she'd actually like to do, instead of rushing to take whatever came first. Maybe she should work in someone else's store to see if owning her own was really a good dream to hold on to. She flipped the eggs over. The truth was she didn't know what she wanted.

Sinclair had probably forgotten all about her. Easy come, easy go. She'd certainly been easy in every way, as far as he was concerned. Every silly magazine article she'd read on the subject said that was a bad idea. Men weren't interested in what was readily available. They'd rather chase after the unattainable. But she had no self-control where Sinclair was concerned.

"Why can't I stop thinking about Sinclair?" Her words echoed off the kitchen walls.

"Because you're in love with him?" Her sister Sheena's voice made her whirl around. She hadn't told anyone, especially Sheena, about her romantic misadventures.

"I am not."

"Are, too." Her sister lolled in the doorway with a big smirk on her face. "You're so secretive, but I've learned to see past your cool expression."

"Why do I feel like I'm thirteen again?" Her big sister always had a superior attitude.

"I have no idea. What I hate is that you still look like you're thirteen. You need more stress in your life."

"Trust me, I have more than enough." She turned the eggs out onto a plate. "Why don't you take some breakfast and leave me alone." She moved to the door and called out, "It's ready."

"Nah. I'll take some breakfast and keep hounding you." She picked up a plate and helped herself to some bacon. "So, is he hot?"

Annie crossed her arms. "I have no idea what you're talking about."

"Yes, you do. You were talking about him when I came in." Her sister's smirk broadened. "So don't try and pretend there isn't anyone. Isn't your boss called Sinclair?"

"He was."

"Then he changed his name to Spike?" Her sister lifted a brow in that infuriating way.

"No. He's still called Sinclair. He's just not my boss anymore." Her stomach dropped a little as she said it. She still couldn't believe her life had turned upside down in such a short time. The loss of her job hadn't sunk in at all, even though it was her who'd quit.

"So, you're in love with him, but he doesn't love you." Sheena picked up a piece of crispy bacon in her fingers and bit it.

"Something like that," she muttered. "I really don't want to talk about it."

"You were talking about it before I came in, so I think you need to get it off your chest. Is he in love with someone else?"

"No. I don't think he's ever been in love with anyone and I don't think he ever will be." She said it with clear conviction that suddenly flooded her brain. "He's been married twice and I don't think he loved either of his wives. I think he was just looking for the right package. I think his whole life is about trying to be organized, efficient and perfect. I don't think he's capable of emotions at all." Her own feelings clawed at her insides.

"Damn. I wasn't sure you were, either, but now I'm beginning to see different." Sheena crunched another piece of bacon. "I always envied you your independence."

"I used to enjoy my independence." Her voice cracked. "And I hope I'll enjoy it again once I get him out of my mind."

"What does he look like?" Her sister lolled in the door frame, munching on her bacon like it was popcorn at the movies.

"What does it matter?" She sat at the table and tried to summon the appetite to eat.

"Is he tall, dark and handsome, by any chance?"

"Yes. Of course." She managed to swallow a bite of eggs. "He's gorgeous."

"Broad shoulders? Tight ass?"

"Go away."

"Does he dress like a preppy country-club type?"

"Yes." She frowned. "How did you know that?"

"Well, I'm describing the guy who's out on the front stoop sweet-talking Granny Pat." She walked in and scooped an egg onto her plate. "Mmm, nice and greasy. Just the way I like 'em."

Annie froze. "What?"

"Bacon grease. Really makes the eggs taste good."

"No. I mean, what did you say about someone talking to Granny?" She could hardly get the words out. She realized she was gripping her knife and fork like weapons.

"This dude drove up in a big shiny car. Asked if an Annie Sullivan lives here." Her sister pretended to be engrossed in her egg.

Annie rose to her feet, almost knocking her chair to the ground. "He's looking for me?"

"Yeah." Sheena chewed slowly, while Annie's blood pressure rose. "He had the address, but you know how our house has no number on it."

Annie raced out of the kitchen. Heart in her throat, she opened the front door and walked out onto the porch. Granny Pat and Sinclair both swiveled to watch her. Her eyes met Sinclair's.

He walked toward her. In a white shirt, open at the collar, and dark pants, he looked dashing and elegant, in stark contrast to the dreary street with its peeling houses and rusting minivans. "Thank God I found you."

His deep voice rocked her and his words chased her soul. He sounded like a lover who'd searched to the ends of the earth for his one and only.

Except that she knew better. "I couldn't stay. Not after the second time."

"This young man has traveled nonstop from California to see you." Granny Pat smiled at him. "Wasn't even sure if you'd be here."

Curiosity pricked her. Sinclair climbed the porch steps in an athletic stride. He stopped just short of her and she could feel the tension radiating off his body. She felt strangely calm. She'd already walked away from him and from their whole affair—you couldn't even call it an affair—and resolved to get on with her life. His sudden appearance on her family's doorstep seemed surreal.

His brows lowered. "I made a terrible mistake."

"Only one?" So cool, her comment seemed to have come from someone else's mouth. Maybe she was angry. Six years of pining followed by two weeks of the greatest pleasure and cruelest torture she could imagine. It could leave any girl on edge.

"I missed you."

I missed you, too. She didn't say it. She hadn't really had the luxury of missing him. She'd been too busy scrambling to reorient her life and figure out what to do next. She knew that if she stopped to think about the life she'd left behind everything would rise up and overwhelm her, so she'd kept her mind and hands busy every minute since she left.

"I couldn't believe you were gone."

"You thought I would just put up with anything you threw at me? I'm pretty tough, but you going back to your ex-wife was too much for me. Not that we had a relationship or anything. I didn't have a chance to develop that illusion." She'd never enjoyed the luxury of thinking she and Sinclair had a future for an entire twenty-four hours. The harsh light of dawn had always managed to dissolve her dream into a mist of memory and regret.

His brow furrowed. "I shouldn't have gone. I should have stayed with you."

"But you didn't." She didn't want to hear his apology. It didn't mean anything now. Whatever they'd shared—so briefly—was over and gone forever. "Everything happens for a reason." His ex must have told him she wasn't interested in getting back together—otherwise he'd probably still be there, trying to do the "honorable thing."

"Diana only wanted money. The baby isn't mine. She had done a DNA test, so she didn't lie about that, but she did lie when she said the baby was mine. The test proved it isn't. I left for the airport as soon as I heard, and I had my mom and Vicki track down your old résumé with your home address on it. You told me your family still lived here and I hoped I'd find you here."

She nodded. Of course. Still, a sliver of pain did prick her. Not so much for her own frustrated longing, but that Sinclair had once again tried to form a bond and been rejected.

Then she wanted to curse herself for caring. What about her own feelings? No one cared about those.

"I have feelings for you, Annie."

His sudden response to her thoughts touched a raw place inside her.

"I've always had feelings for you, Sinclair. They've brought me nothing but pain."

Emotion flickered over his chiseled features. "I know I'm to blame. I've been blind for so long."

She wanted to agree with him. But what would that accomplish? The pained expression in his eyes tugged at her heartstrings. Even now, after everything that had happened, she ached to run into his arms and tell him how happy she was to see him. He'd come all the way to Connecticut to find her. And apparently to reveal his true feelings for her.

But why? Would he beg her to come back and jump between the sheets with him? Or did he need her to take care of his house and his mother? She had no intention of doing either. "What do you want from me, Sinclair?"

Annie bit her lip and steeled herself to say no to whatever he hoped to talk her into.

Sinclair reached into the pocket of his pants. Annie's eyes grew wider as he pulled out a large, sparkling ring.

Annie felt her legs grow wobbly. Surely he wasn't...?

He was going to propose. Thoughts swirled around Annie's mind like hurricane-force winds. Years of idle dreaming and foolish fantasy were coalescing in this crazy moment on the front porch. The man of her dreams held a sparkling diamond the size of a muscatel grape and was about to ask her to be his wife.

And she was about to say no.

With an expression of intense concentration, Sinclair held the ring between his thumb and forefinger. She heard his intake of breath as he looked up to meet her eyes. "Annie, will you marry me?"

Eleven

The ring felt hard and sharp between Sinclair's finger and thumb. The sun, high overhead, hit its faceted surface, throwing out daggers of light. His words hung in the air as the seconds stretched out and he waited for her response.

Not the smile he'd hoped for. Nor the sigh, or the embarrassed laugh. Instead, his beautiful Annie looked... pained.

"Maybe you two need some privacy." Her grandmother's voice penetrated the slight fog of disbelief that accompanied her lack of response. Her broad chin lowered its tilt slightly. Then her cheerful expression darkened and she peered at Annie. "Is there something I should know?" She gave a pointed look at Annie's waist.

"No!" Annie's lightning-fast response made his neurons snap. Her abrupt refusal felt like a slap, and a response to his proposal, even though she was only replying to her grandmother's question. "Let's go inside." She didn't look at him.

Still holding the ring, he followed her through the front door. Another girl about Annie's age stood nearby, but Annie didn't introduce her. She walked down the hallway and he followed her into a large living room with high ceilings. She gestured for him to sit, and he lowered himself onto the worn, overstuffed sofa. She sat on an armchair about ten feet away, and the distance between them felt wide as Long Island Sound.

The ring stuck out, still throbbing with light, a sore thumb of frustrated hope and wounded feelings. "You must think my proposal is premature, because we haven't really...dated."

"Yes, that's true." She blinked. Her expression was blank, as if she didn't feel any of the emotion that crashed and sloshed around in him like the ocean in a gale. "You don't really know me."

"But I do." Hope surged in his chest at the chance to explain himself. "I've known you for six years. I feel closer to you after that one night we spent together than to anyone else in my life. Surely you feel the connection between us."

He saw emotion light her blue eyes. "Yes, I felt it." She frowned. "But that doesn't mean we're meant to be together. We don't have anything in common. If I wasn't your employee we'd never have even met."

"We have a lot in common." He spoke quietly. "It's my fault for being oblivious to it for years, but I can see now that we look at the world in a very similar way."

"I guess that's why I've done such a good job of running your house the way you like it." He wanted to agree heartily, but the way she said it sounded more like an accusation than an agreement.

"I don't want you to run my house anymore. I want you to run my life."

Her eyes widened. "Like a glorified personal assistant?"

"No." Frustration ripped through him. Why was he such a disaster when it came to matters of the heart? A bull in a china shop was subtle by comparison. "I want you to be my life partner, my constant companion... my soul mate."

She sat there, so sad and still. The surface of her eyes suggested emotion traveling behind them, but her face revealed nothing. "You can't become someone's soul mate. If we were soul mates we'd have realized it a long time ago."

He closed his fist around the ring and squeezed until the facets dug into his palm. He cursed himself for being an idiot. How had he managed to live for six years with the perfect woman under his roof—or at least one of his roofs—and not realized she was the one he'd been waiting for?

Instead he'd been dating—and marrying—people who were all wrong.

"Never mind the mumbo jumbo about soul mates." He leaned forward, urgency spurring his muscles. "I want you, Annie. Something deep inside me, I don't know what it's called—" He thumped his chest with his clenched fist, driving the ring harder against his hurting flesh. "Something tells me I need you. I don't want to go home without you." His words rang with all the raw emotion that soaked through him, and he prayed she'd feel the urgency and truth of his words.

A sudden tear sparkled in one of her eyes, filled her lower lid for a moment, then dropped across her cheek. His chest ached. Had he hurt her further with all his declarations?

She still said nothing.

"What is it, Annie? Have I said the wrong thing?" He heard his own voice crack.

"We're from totally different backgrounds. As you can see." She made a wooden gesture indicating the room. Her voice sounded flat. Only her eyes betrayed any emotion beneath the surface.

"Our backgrounds aren't important at all. All my life I've tried to make a relationship work with women from backgrounds identical to mine, and look how that turned out. Where you come from doesn't matter. It's what you want to accomplish in your life, how you want to live it and who you want to share it with that counts."

Her eyes were dry, that single tear now only a bright trail across her cheek. She stared at him for a moment without blinking. Then she looked away, past him. "It wouldn't work."

"Why not?" He sprang to his feet. Why couldn't he make her see sense?

Annie looked at him quietly for a moment. "Because you don't love me."

Her words dropped like a stone to his heart. Had he said all these things, even asked her to marry him, without once telling her that he loved her?

"I do love you." He drew in a breath to the bottom of his lungs. "I love you with all my heart." He strode across the room and crouched at her feet. Unable to resist, he snatched her hands out of her lap and held them. The big ring tumbled to the floor. "I didn't know what love was until I took you in my arms. I feel like I've been skating over the surface of life until now. I thought I was seeing life in color and smelling its scents and hearing its music, but I wasn't. I've been watching life on television, and suddenly I'm alive and can feel and see and taste all those things I've watched from afar for so long."

He heard his voice getting loud. Her hands trembled in his and he held them closer. "I've never felt this way before, or even knew that I could. It's taken me all this time to figure out what's going on with me. When I got to California I felt like someone had cut my heart out with a knife. All I could think about was coming back to you." His chest swelled with emotion. "Because I love you, Annie. I do love you."

Twin tears sprang to her eyes and rolled down her cheeks. "I believe you. I really do." Her voice trembled. "Oh, Sinclair. If only I believed we could be happy together."

"Never mind about that." He held her hands tight as hope soared in his heart. "We could be unhappy together. As long as we're together. I can't bear to be without you, Annie."

She laughed, and the light that had dimmed returned to her eyes, a brilliant sparkle that made the diamond now lying somewhere on the floor seem like a chunk of old glass by comparison. "You know, now you're making some sense. Being unhappy together actually sounds achievable."

"Better than being unhappy apart." He felt laughter bubbling in his chest. "And who knows, maybe we'll learn to smile from time to time."

"I wouldn't divorce you, you know." Her face wore

that strange, calm expression again. She had an air of
total self-assurance that filled his heart with joy.

"I wouldn't let you." He softened his fierce grip
on her hands long enough to lift them to his lips. The
scent of her skin made him tremble. "Damn, Annie.
I've missed you so much it hurts."

"I've missed you, too." Emotion glistened in her
gaze. "I didn't want to admit it. It was just one more
thing to keep to myself. Kind of like falling in love with
you over the past six years."

"I could kick myself for wasting so much time. I
promise I'll make it up to you. If you'll give me the
chance."

She bit her lip, which shone red against her pale skin.
"I am feeling reckless today."

"Wait. Let me start over. Don't move a muscle." Still
holding both her hands in one of his, he groped toward
the floor with the other. His fingers met the cold metal
of the ring and he snatched it back up. "You never did
answer my question." He hesitated for a moment, gathering the strength to ask again. "Annie Sullivan, I love
you in a way I never dreamed possible, and I want to
spend the rest of my life at your side. Will you marry
me?"

"I will." She said it quickly and quietly, eyes sparkling bright.

He felt like letting out a cheer. Instead he slid the en-
gagement ring onto her finger. The fit was snug, perfect.

"What a stunning ring." She stared at it. "Those look
like rubies." The big, cushion-cut diamond was ringed
by smaller, dark pink stones.

"I believe so. It's a Drummond family ring, so it

might be cursed, but it's not as if we're trying to be happy together."

She looked at him, eyes sparkling with humor. "Yes, that is a relief. Really takes the pressure off. How horribly did the last person to wear it die?"

"Hmm." He pretended to consider. "Actually she's still alive. My mom said it's too beautiful to sit in a safe, so she suggested I give it to you."

"Your mom knew you were going to propose to me?" Her eyes grew huge.

"She made me promise not to screw it up." He squeezed her hands gently, taking care not to crush the ring against her skin. "She said she won't speak to me if I come back without you."

Annie stared, blinking, her lips slightly parted. The urge to kiss her swelled inside him. "You did say yes, didn't you?" He spoke softly, afraid to break the spell that seemed to bind them together.

"Yes, yes I did." Her mouth held him riveted, soft and lush, saying the words he needed to hear. His lips met hers and their arms wound around each other. The feel of her body in his arms made a sigh rise through his chest, where it got lost in their kiss. Having Annie in his arms felt so right. He could stay right here and kiss her forever.

A knock sounded at the door, and he managed to pull away from Annie enough to look behind him and see the source. "Come in?" It was more a question than a command. The door opened slowly to reveal the rather red faces of her grandmother and a woman about Annie's age.

"Were you listening at the keyhole?" Annie jumped to her feet.

Her grandmother scrambled slowly upright, with the help of the door frame. "I needed to make sure he wasn't taking advantage of you." She pushed her glasses back up her nose.

"And what's your excuse?" Annie asked of the younger woman.

"Curiosity." A sly smile crept across her face. "And we were right to be curious. It got pretty interesting."

Annie put her hands on her hips. "So I suppose there's no need for me to make an announcement of any kind."

They looked from her to Sinclair and back. "We'd still like one." Her grandmother looked cheerfully expectant.

"Annie and I would like to announce that we're getting married."

"Can I be maid of honor?"

Annie had her arms around his waist. "Sinclair, this is my sister, Sheena. Sheena, we didn't say that we're having a big wedding. Just that we're getting married. For myself I'd prefer as little pomp and ceremony as possible."

"What's this I hear about someone getting married?" A short, plump man appeared behind the women.

Annie's grandmother stared at him. "Oh, my lord, the excitement has drawn your father away from his television. Wonders will never cease. Your daughter's getting married." She gestured to Sinclair. "To this fine young man." She leaned toward him. "His BMW is parked outside."

Her father blinked and scratched his forehead. "Goodness. I break from my show for a plate of eggs, and now I've lost the plot entirely. I suppose congratulations are in order." He stepped forward and shook Sinclair by the hand.

"I promise you I'll take good care of her."

"I'm not sure I need taking care of. I'm usually the one taking care of everyone else," Annie protested.

"Then it's time you took a break." Sinclair slid his arm around her waist. "And I think you should start with a nice, long vacation."

Annie shoved her belongings back into her flimsy suitcase again. It wasn't hard to convince Sinclair that they needed to visit his mom before flying off to parts unknown. Katherine Drummond was still in a vulnerable state and the events of the last week were enough to stress even a healthy person.

She splashed water on her face before heading back down into the maelstrom of her family. Her mom had come home from work and screamed when she heard the news. They'd all crowded around Sinclair's car and left fingerprints on the shiny paint. He'd handled their probing questions with grace and charm, but she couldn't wait to get out of here and back to the relative calm of Dog Harbor.

But how would it feel to be there as a guest instead of an employee? Not even a guest. What was she?

"I feel very old-fashioned, like I've come to carry you away from your family and take you back to my castle." Sinclair stood in the doorway. "I'm sure the Drummond ancestors would approve."

"And I didn't even have to lay seige. If only we could sail my car across Long Island Sound we'd be there in about fifteen minutes. Shame we actually have about a four-hour drive."

* * *

Scenery whipped by outside the window as they talked about Sinclair's other houses, the ones she'd never seen: the ski chalet in Colorado, an old beach-front mansion in northern California, and the hunting lodge in upper Michigan. They decided to be married in the garden of Dog Harbor, preferably within the month, with only people they considered true friends in attendance.

When they pulled into the driveway, the house looked different. She couldn't put her finger on what had changed. The chimneys still loomed above the gabled roof, windows sparkled in the late afternoon sun, and the lawn glowed green on either side of the gravel drive.

"Welcome home," Sinclair whispered in her ear. "Look. No one's here but us. I told my mom and Vicki to make themselves scarce for a few days. We have some catching up to do."

"I know what you mean. We're short at least six months of dating."

"We'll make up for lost time." His sultry gaze made her shiver. Desire and anticipation roared through her at the prospect of being alone with Sinclair—her new fiancé.

She still couldn't believe it.

"Don't move. I need to carry you over the threshold." Sinclair had rounded the circular drive and pulled up in front of the house. He leaped from the car and opened her door before she had time to protest. Dangling the key in his teeth, he slid his arms under her and lifted her out of the car. She gave a little scream as he ran for the house. "You don't mind if I hurry, do you? I'm feeling impatient."

"Not at all." She clung to his neck as he bounded up the stairs, and fumbled with the keys while balancing her in one strong arm.

She whispered in his ear. "Where's the housekeeper when you need her?"

"She's indisposed." He kicked open the door and threw his keys on the sideboard, then carried her over the marble threshold into the wide foyer. "On a permanent basis." His hot breath tickled her skin, sending ripples of sensation to her toes.

"Hey, what's that?" Something sitting in the middle of the dining room table had caught her eye as he headed past on the way to the stairs.

"What?"

"Take a detour into the dining room. I think there's a note on the table."

"It better be a short one," he growled playfully. "I have other priorities." He swung into the dining room, nuzzling her cheek. "What the heck is that?" A scarred wooden box sat in the middle of the table. Next to it, a sheet of white paper was scrawled with the words, *We found it.*

"The cup? I think you'd better put me down."

"What if I don't want to put you down?" He kissed her ear, and heat flooded her core. "I have more important things to do than mess with an old cup." He lifted her onto the dining room table, and kissed her with force. All the excitement that had built up during their long drive blossomed into the longest and fiercest kiss she'd ever known. Sinclair's powerful fingers plucked at the buttons on her shirt and soon slid it back over her shoulders. She tugged his polo shirt over his head, revealing his hard chest with that intoxicating sprinkling of dark hair that led below his belt buckle. Her fingers fumbled with the buckle while Sinclair breathed kisses over her face and neck, and licked her nipples into hard peaks.

Her belly trembled under his touch as he unzipped her pants and slid them down over her legs, leaving her sitting on the polished antique table in her bikini underwear. She giggled. "Should we really be doing this here?"

"Absolutely." Sinclair stepped out of his pants. The force of his desire was clearly visible and only heightened her own. Lips gently pressed to hers, he entered her slowly but surely, filling her and making her gasp with pleasure. The table proved surprisingly sturdy as Sinclair took them both on a sensual journey at its edge. Then, just as she felt her climax draw near, he lifted her up and carried her, striding swiftly, into the formal living room, where he spread her on the brocade chaise longue.

"I think we're scandalizing the furniture." She sighed at the sensation of sinking into the soft, upholstered surface, with Sinclair's warm, heavy weight on top of her.

"It could use some excitement." He licked her lips, making her gasp. "I know I needed some."

He sank deeper, and she melted under him, giving herself over to the sensation that lapped through her. For once she didn't have to worry about what would happen next, or what kind of a terrible mistake she was making. She was meant to be here, right now, in Sinclair's arms. Her heart felt so full. All the hope and fear she'd been storing for so long spilled over into passion. She gripped Sinclair as they moved together, rising and falling with him and holding him as tight as she could until their climax threw them deep into the chaise, breathing in heavy unison.

"Am I dreaming?" she said, when she could finally catch enough breath.

"If you are, I am, too. Let's not wake up." His eyelashes brushed her cheek as he lay against her.

"We never looked in the box."

"What box?" His chest rose and fell and beads of perspiration stood out on his proud forehead. "Oh, yes. That box. I'm sure whatever it is can wait."

"Apparently we couldn't." She bit her lip, trying to stop a smile sneaking across her face.

"Speak for yourself. I could have easily gone for a cool dip in the Sound instead." His eyes opened just enough for her to see them twinkle with mischief.

"Liar." She slid a fingertip down the groove of his spine and he shivered slightly in response. "But I'm glad you have no self-control where I'm concerned. Otherwise we might have gone on tiptoeing around each other for another six years."

"That would have been a tragedy." He grazed her cheek with his teeth. "Come on. Let's go see what the big mystery is." He climbed off the sofa and pulled her gently to her feet. She insisted on grabbing a couple of white linen tablecloths from the pantry on the way back to the dining room, so they looked like ancient Romans as they surveyed the aged wooden box again.

Sinclair stood back. "You first. You're the newest member of the Drummond family."

"Not yet."

"Doesn't matter. The curse starts working as soon

as you agree to marry a Drummond." A sneaky dimple appeared in his cheek.

"All right. Since I'm doomed anyway." She lifted the lid, which creaked loudly. Inside was a moth-eaten piece of tartan cloth, folded around something. She pulled the object out—it was heavy—and held it in her hands. She placed it on the table and peeled back the cloth, sending a small cloud of dust into the air. Her nose tickled with the desire to sneeze. The cloth fell away to reveal a very dark, tarnished rod of metal. "Huh? That's not what I was expecting. I thought it would be one-third of the infamous cup."

"Maybe it is." Sinclair reached into the folds of the fabric and drew it out. The surface was scored with patterns, and each end had a sort of claw on it. "This could be the stem."

"And the other pieces are the base and the cup? I never thought of that." He placed the cool metal rod in her hands, and she turned it. "These ends do look like they could attach to something else. I wonder where they found it?"

"I wonder *when* they found it. And if it coincides with me finally having the good sense to pursue the one woman I need by my side." He looked at her, his dark gaze serious. Her heart fluttered at the depth of emotion she read in his face.

"I love you, Sinclair."

"I love you, too, and thank heaven I had the sense to realize that before it was too late. Welcome home, Annie." He laid another warm kiss on her lips. "And welcome to the ancient line of Drummonds."

Epilogue

"Katherine, you shouldn't have." Annie pulled tissue paper from the big box. "It's not even Christmas yet."

"I don't have to wait for special occasions to give my grandson a few things." The balsam tree she and Sinclair had cut and brought home together already had piles of wrapped boxes and gift bags that reached as high as its lower branches.

"It might help if you wait until your grandson is actually born." Sinclair's gruff voice moved behind her as he slid his arms around Annie's waist—which was growing larger every day. Her skin tingled under his affectionate touch, even through her winter clothes.

"I'm naturally impatient, darling. You know that. And Annie understands, don't you?"

Annie pulled yet another adorable tiny outfit—French, of course—with a pattern of little sailboats, from the box. Followed by a matching hat and booties.

"Of course I do. It's impossible not to be excited about the arrival of a new person in our midst."

"The newest Drummond shall want for nothing. Do you think it would be silly to buy a sled in the sales?" Snow had been falling steadily for two days and they were all snowed into a very quiet and sleepy Dog Harbor.

"Definitely silly." Sinclair laughed. "He won't be able to sled until at least the winter after next. Besides, we found about eight antique sleds up in the attic. Those are probably faster and sturdier than anything you'll find in a toy store."

"I'm just so excited. It's hard to stop myself. I'm sure I'll calm down once the doctor gives me the okay to travel again. He said to wait a full year since my illness. That's another four months! It's driving me to distraction that I can't fly to Scotland and shake the young laird into looking for more of the cup."

"Why can't you go to Florida and harass the Drummond down there?" Sinclair kissed Annie gently on the cheek as she folded the baby outfit and laid it on the sofa. "That's only a domestic flight."

"Vicki insisted on going." Katherine shrugged her slim shoulders. "She seemed really interested. I think she knows people down there."

"Or she wants to win the reward she convinced you to offer for finding the cup piece." Sinclair topped up their glasses of eggnog.

"Sinclair! Vicki doesn't need money. Her family made a fortune in…something or other. I forget what."

"Never mind. I hope she does find it. I think more Drummonds deserve to be as happy as we are."

"See, I knew you could be happily married. You just

needed to pick the right woman." Katherine beamed at Annie.

"That's what I told him myself." Annie smiled at Sinclair.

"And I've never seen the house look so glorious at Christmastime." Fragrant pine decorated the balusters and fireplaces, and ornaments of all kinds had been brought out of the attic and polished before finding their new places in the house and on the tree.

"That's because we usually go to the Colorado house." Annie surveyed her handiwork. She'd always dreamed of decorating the house for Christmas. Like the lovely wedding they'd held on the lawn under fall-spangled trees, it was a dream come true. Sometimes her heart felt so full it was hard to keep her emotions contained. Or maybe that was just the pregnancy hormones. "Next year will be even more special, when we have a child to share it with."

Katherine rose from her seat and hugged Annie with tears in her eyes. "You've made me so happy already." She turned to Sinclair. "And I should scold you for making myself and Annie wait so long for you to come to your senses."

Sinclair sipped his eggnog. "I'm a slow study. I get there in the end, though. I can't believe I never thought of living here full-time before."

"The house feels quite different now it's a real home." Annie smiled at the warm and festive living room. "Before I felt a bit like I was always getting ready for a theatrical production."

"Now you're just living in one every day." Sinclair winked.

"Nonsense." Katherine reached for a walnut and the

ornate Victorian nutcracker. "Annie's kept everything very low-key and tasteful."

"I love being surrounded by all the beautiful old things the family has gathered over the years. This is such a special place. I suppose that's why the Drummonds have always kept it."

"I look forward to spending the rest of my life here." Sinclair slid his arm around her shoulders, sending a shiver of warmth through her. "With you."

Annie sighed. "Me, too. Leaving this house was almost as hard as leaving you." She nudged him. "I can happily stay here forever."

"Sinclair told me you're planning to open a shop." Katherine peeled her cracked walnut and ate it with delicate fingers.

"Yes." She smiled at Sinclair, butterflies still rising in her stomach at the thought of her grand plan. "It's going to sell local handmade crafts and foods. I plan to make some of them myself, too. I won't open for another year, though. I'm still taking business classes and developing my plan." She patted her belly. "And I'll be very busy for a while."

"I knew finding the cup would change our luck." Katherine glowed with satisfaction. She seemed to have fully recovered from her illness. "Where is our piece, by the way? I still don't know how we figured out that was a stem. It was just rattling around in the bottom of that box with a bunch of eighteenth-century tobacco pipes. It wouldn't look good if we track down the other two and we'd lost ours again."

Annie laughed. "It's up on the fireplace next to that glass bottle."

"Why do you have an empty wine bottle on the mantel?"

She shrugged. "It washed ashore one day and we decided to keep it." She and Sinclair had been walking on the beach one morning, looking out over the Sound and talking about the future, when they'd spotted a wine bottle bobbing in the surf. Sinclair had waded in to grab it and—surprise, surprise!—there were two tiny pieces of paper rolled up in the bottom.

The paper had been washed completely clean by water leaking in through a cracked cork, so while they were certain it was debris from the party they'd attended, they had no idea if it was their own fond wishes that had rinsed off or someone else's. They resolved to put their thoughts into words.

Sinclair had said "Annie, I never knew what I was looking for until I found you in my arms." And she told him of her hope that he would live happily ever after, preferably with her. They'd put the mysterious notes back into the bottle and placed it up high next to the cup piece that had—just maybe?—lifted centuries of bad luck and finally brought them together.

* * * * *

#2173 AN INCONVENIENT AFFAIR
The Alpha Brotherhood
Catherine Mann
To fix a long-neglected injustice, this bad-boy-turned-good begins an affair with the woman who has every reason to mistrust him most.

#2174 EXQUISITE ACQUISITIONS
The Highest Bidder
Charlene Sands
A runaway Hollywood starlet seeks refuge at Carter McCay's ranch but soon finds herself falling for the man who's sworn to never love again.

#2175 PRINCESS IN THE MAKING
Billionaires and Babies
Michelle Celmer
Prince Marcus considers himself a noble man...until he falls in love with the woman his father is determined to marry.

#2176 THE RELUCTANT HEIRESS
Lone Star Legacy
Sara Orwig
When an heiress refuses her inheritance, can a trusted family friend win her over without falling in love?

#2177 A CASE OF KISS AND TELL
Matchmakers, Inc.
Katherine Garbera
She will stop at nothing to get the story; he will stop at nothing to get her into his bed.

#2178 A PERFECT HUSBAND
The Pearl House
Fiona Brand
A woman on the hunt for a husband falls into an affair with a former lover, who she thinks is the wrong man for her.

You can find more information on upcoming Harlequin®
titles, free excerpts and more at www.Harlequin.com.

HDCNM0712

Montana. Home of big blue skies, wide open spaces...and really hot men! Join bestselling author Debbi Rawlins in celebrating all things Western in Harlequin® Blaze™ with her new miniseries, MADE IN MONTANA!

Read on for a sneak peek of
BAREFOOT BLUE JEAN NIGHT

"OVER HERE," Cole said.

Jamie headed toward him, her lips rising in a cheeky grin. "What makes you think I'm looking for you?"

He drew her back into the shadows inside the barn. "Then tell me, Jamie, what are you looking for?"

A spark had ignited between them and she had the distinct feeling that tonight was the night for fireworks—despite the threat of thieves. The only unanswered question was when.

"Oh, I get it," she said finally. "You're trying to distract me from telling you I'm going to help you keep watch."

He lowered both hands. "No, you're not."

"I am. Rachel thinks it's an excellent idea."

He shot a frown toward the kitchen. "I don't care what my sister thinks. You have five minutes, then you're marching right back into that house."

She wasn't about to let him get away with pulling back. Not to mention she didn't care for his bossiness. "You're such a coward."

"Let's put it this way..." He arched a brow. "How much watching do you think we'd get done?"

She flattened a palm on his chest. His heart pounded as hard as hers. "I see your point. But no, I won't be a good little girl and do as you so charmingly ordered."

"It wasn't an order," he muttered. "It was a strongly

worded request. I have to stay alert out here."

"Correct. That's why we'll behave like adults and refrain from making out."

"Making out," he repeated with a snort. "Haven't heard that term in a while." Then he caught her wrist and pulled her hand away from his chest. "Not a good start."

"It's barely dark. No one's going to sneak in now. Once we seriously need to pay attention, I'll be as good as gold. But I figure we have at least an hour."

"For?"

"Oh, I don't know…" With the tip of her finger she traced his lower lip. "Nothing too risky. Just some kissing. Maybe I'll even let you get to first base."

Cole laughed. "Honey, I've never stopped at first base before and I'm not about to start now."

Don't miss BAREFOOT BLUE JEAN NIGHT
by Debbi Rawlins.

Available August 2012 from Harlequin® Blaze™
wherever books are sold.

HBEXP0812